For more than forty years,
Yearling has been the leading name
in classic and award-winning literature
for young readers.

Yearling books feature children's
favorite authors and characters,
providing dynamic stories of adventure,
humor, history, mystery, and fantasy.

Trust Yearling paperbacks to entertain,
inspire, and promote the love of reading
in all children.

OTHER YEARLING BOOKS YOU WILL ENJOY

SONG OF SAMPO LAKE, *William Durbin*

WINTERING, *William Durbin*

THE BROKEN BLADE, *William Durbin*

TADPOLE, *Ruth White*

MR. TUCKET, *Gary Paulsen*

TUCKET'S RIDE, *Gary Paulsen*

TUCKET'S GOLD, *Gary Paulsen*

DEAR LEVI: LETTERS FROM THE OVERLAND TRAIL
Elvira Woodruff

THUNDER ROLLING IN THE MOUNTAINS, *Scott O'Dell*

VARJAK PAW, *SF Said*

To Amy

BLACKWATER BEN

WILLIAM DURBIN

W. Durbin

12 - 18 - 07

A YEARLING BOOK

Published by Yearling, an imprint of Random House Children's Books
a division of Random House, Inc., New York

Visit us on the Web! www.randomhouse.com/kids

Educators and librarians, for a variety of teaching tools, visit us at
www.randomhouse.com/teachers

ISBN: 0-440-42008-3

Reprinted by arrangement with Wendy Lamb Books

Printed in the United States of America

July 2005

5 4 3

TO BARBARA JO,
AGAIN AND ALWAYS

Logging Camp Glossary, or Lumberjack Lingo

What does it mean when a lumberjack says, "The groundhogs are sending a blue butt up to the sky hook"? Use this glossary of logging camp terms to find out.

BARN BOSS: Cares for the horses and maintains the horse barn.

BLACKJACK: Coffee.

BLUE BUTT: Pine log with a big "bell" at one end. It is dangerous to load because it can easily spin out of control.

BOILING-UP SHACK: Place to bathe and do laundry. Rarely used.

BULL COOK: General maintenance man of the camp. Also in charge of the bunkhouse.

CALKS, CAULKS, OR CORKS: Sharp spikes set in the soles of loggers' boots. Also, the spikes in the horses' shoes.

COOK: Head cook. Orders the food, supervises the kitchen staff, and plans all the meals.

COOKEE: Cook's helper.

CUT: Area of the woods where the loggers are harvesting timber.

DEACON'S BENCH: Seat built at the foot of each bunk.

DENTIST OR FILER: Sharpens the teeth on the crosscut saws.

FORGE: Furnace for heating metal to be wrought or welded.

FOUR-HORSE TEAMSTER: Hauls the logs to the landing.

GAZEBO: Greenhorn or beginner.

GRAYBACKS: Lice. Also known as traveling dandruff, blue jackets, and crumbs.

GROUNDHOG OR SENDING-UP MAN: Helps guide the logs onto the hauling sleds.

IRON MAN: Blacksmith. Repairs the steel and iron in camp. Also makes and fits horseshoes.

LANDING: Area where logs are piled before being transported by rail, river, or road to the sawmill.

LOG DRIVER OR RIVER RAT: Helps drive the logs downriver to the mill after the spring breakup.

MISERY WHIP: Two-man crosscut saw used by sawyers to fell trees.

NOTCHER OR UNDERCUTTER: Notches the trees with an ax to determine in which direction they will fall.

PENCIL PUSHER: Camp clerk. Keeps the payroll, orders supplies, and manages the camp store.

PUSH: Foreman.

ROAD MONKEY: Helps with road maintenance, shoveling road apples (manure) off the ice roads, and haying the hills.

SAWYERS OR FELLERS: Work in pairs, using a crosscut saw to fell trees.

SHOEPACK PIE: Pie made out of vinegar, cornstarch, and sugar, sometimes flavored with lemon extract or vanilla.

SKID MAN OR SKIDDING TEAMSTER: Skids the logs out of the woods to the edge of the ice roads.

SKY HOOK OR TOP LOADER: Aristocrat of the logging camp. In charge of loading the logs onto the hauling sleds.

SKY PILOT: Minister who travels from camp to camp.

SNOOZE: Snuff. A tobacco product. Also known as Scandihoovian dynamite, galloping dust, Swedish brain food.

SWAMPER: Clears the trails for the skid men and saws the logs into sixteen-foot lengths after they are felled.

SWAMP WATER: Tea.

SWINGDINGLE: Lunch sleigh that is used to haul food to the loggers working at the cut.

TOTE TEAMSTER: Drives a wagon or a sleigh to and from town, delivering supplies to the logging camps.

WANIGAN: Floating cookshack that follows the log drivers.

WATER TANK CREW: Pulls a sled-mounted wooden water tank down the road to build up the ice ruts.

WOOD BUTCHER: Carpenter. Also does harness work.

Daylight in the Swamp
Blackwater Logging Camp, 1898

"**D**aylight in the swamp!" Pa yelled. Ben groaned and turned over. Pa's voice had two volumes: loud and louder. Ben squinted in the lantern light. Pa's square shoulders filled the doorway of the bunk room. "Roll out or roll up," he said.

Ben scrambled to pull on his wool pants and socks. Before he had tied his boots, he heard Pa lift the lid of the kitchen range and chuck in a stick of wood. "Hey, cookee, our bread will never rise if we don't get it warmed up in here," Pa called.

Ben buttoned his shirt and looked at his pocket watch. It was quarter past four. His eyes burned from woodsmoke as he stepped from the bunk room into the kitchen. He hurried over and added wood to the potbellied stove. Then he filled a washbasin from the pail of water on top of the range and splashed his hands and face. But when he reached for a towel, Pa said, "Don't forget the soap."

The second cook's helper, Skip, smirked like he always did whenever Pa corrected Ben.

Ben hustled to the counter to help. "About time you got here." Pa didn't look up from the bean pot he was stirring. "Ain't you forgetting something?"

"I washed my hands."

When Ben saw Skip grin again, he remembered that he hadn't put on his apron. "Sorry, Pa," Ben said, reaching for the wooden rack where they hung the towels and aprons.

"Sorry won't cut it if these lumberjacks get sick from a dirty kitchen." Pa wouldn't let Ben or Skip near the food without scrubbing their hands and tying on their aprons, and he insisted that they wear white shirts. "I seen cookees come straight from the barn without washing. We ain't gonna have that in this camp."

"It wasn't like I was out feeding the horses," Ben said, knowing it was wrong to argue but not being able to stop himself.

"You forgot the rules."

"But—"

"Everybody in this cookshack follows my rules." Pa set down his spoon. "Am I clear?" Pa had learned his cooking in the army, and he was a stickler for rules. Skip was grinning bigger now.

"Yes, sir," Ben said.

"What are the two questions a jack always asks before he signs on at a logging camp?" Pa asked. Pa was one of the few lumberjacks without a beard, and his clean-shaven jaw was tight. His hair was neatly parted down the middle and slicked back.

"Well?" Pa said.

Skip jumped in. "He asks, 'Who's the cook?'"

"And 'Who's the foreman?'" Ben added.

"Say push, stupid, not foreman," Skip said.

"That's right," Pa said, putting the lid back on the bean pot. "Nobody wants to spend a winter in the woods with a dirty hash slinger or an ornery push. There's only two things these jacks can look forward to: mealtime and springtime."

"And mealtime comes a whole lot sooner," Skip said, finishing one of Pa's favorite sayings.

"Which is what makes our job so important," Pa added, beaming.

No matter how often Pa told Ben to be proud of his cookee's duties, greasing pans, frying flapjacks, cleaning lamp chimneys, and washing dishes were not Ben's idea of important jobs. Last fall when Pa asked Ben to work at the Blackwater Logging Camp, Ben had imagined himself felling giant pines and driving a four-horse team. So far the closest he'd gotten to holding reins was tying his apron strings.

Ben started the oatmeal boiling and opened a gallon-sized can of stewed prunes. The men called prunes logging berries, and they insisted on having them at every meal. Baked beans were also served for breakfast, lunch, and dinner. Ben set four pans of sowbelly in the oven to brown. Then he helped Pa mix up the batter for his sour-dough flapjacks, known as sweat pads.

As soon as breakfast was ready, Pa said, "Fetch me the Gabriel horn." Ben took down the five-foot-long tin horn from its hook on the log wall and handed it to Pa. Steam rushed in as Pa stepped through the door and blew into the bugle-style mouthpiece.

Before the third blast had echoed over the clearing, the bunkhouse door swung open and Packy Peloquin stepped out. Tucking in his wool shirt and tying a bright red sash around his middle—the other lumberjacks wore suspenders—Packy trotted toward the cookshack. "Look who's up," Pa said, knowing that Packy was the first in line for every meal. He was barely five feet tall, but he ate so much that Pa teased him about having a hollow leg.

Unlike most of the jacks, Packy was always friendly. "*Bonjour*, Benjamin," he said, smiling, but the moment he stepped inside the cookshack, he was quiet. The jacks were allowed to wave an empty platter and call for more food, but table talk was forbidden. Anyone who violated Pa's rule missed the next meal.

Skip was scraping the fried spuds onto a platter, and Ben was about to scoop the last batch of doughnuts out of the big cast-iron frying pan when he heard a yell out the back door. "Was that Pa?" Ben asked.

"He just stepped outside to go to the root cellar," Skip said. "I hope he didn't hurt hisself."

Ben was used to Pa's shouting, but the only time he had heard Pa yell that loudly was when he'd plowed over a wasps' nest.

Skip pushed the back door open and ran to the root cellar.

Ben lit a lantern and followed. At the cellar, he heard

Skip say, "I'm real sorry, Mr. Ward. I meant to close the syrup spigot, but—"

"But nothing!" Pa roared.

Ben noticed a sweet scent as he walked down the steps. Pa's face was flushed, and amber liquid dripped from his hands. He'd tripped and fallen into an inch-deep puddle of maple syrup.

"I'll teach you a lesson." Pa grabbed at Skip, and the cookee trampled Ben's feet as he ran up the stairs. "Come back here, you laggard pup."

"Don't, Pa," Ben called, but Pa brushed past him. Ben raced up the steps and out of the cellar, but Skip was already scooting into the cookshack with Pa only two strides behind. "Pa," Ben yelled, but he might as well have been shouting at the wall.

When Ben opened the back door, the air was filled with black smoke. The doughnuts were on fire. While Pa chased Skip toward the front door, Ben ran to the wood range and slid the pan aside. Then he turned.

Twenty openmouthed lumberjacks had cleared a path down the middle of the cookshack. They were lined up like they were watching a race at a Fourth of July picnic. A row of sticky footprints led across the floor. Pa's apron flapped to one side, and he was waving a soup ladle at Skip as he ran. "Wait till I get my hands on you, you little pipsqueak."

Pa hit top speed just as Arno Edwards, the blacksmith, opened the front door. Arno, who was half asleep, made the mistake of watching Skip leap off the steps. He turned, and Pa and Arno crashed belly to belly and pitched off the steps and onto the ground.

Pa was covered with snow when he got up. He yelled, "You better run, you pup, you." Then he reached down and helped Arno up. Arno looked at his syrup-coated hand and mumbled, "Thanks, I guess."

The men in the cookshack burst out laughing. "What's so funny?" Pa marched back inside. "Haven't you ever seen a—"

"You mean haven't we ever seen a man take a bath in maple syrup?" interrupted the push, Bob Collins.

Pa said, "Ben, you see these boys get their breakfast. I've got to clean up a little."

As Pa filled a washbasin at the back counter, Ben set out the serving platters. The push lent a hand in carrying out the oatmeal and fried spuds and sowbelly.

The jacks normally ate without so much as a whisper, but today they couldn't help chuckling.

By the time Pa had put on a clean white shirt, the jacks had left for the cut. Ben was hoping Pa would appreciate how he'd saved the meal and see how funny it all was, but Pa only said to the push, "You gonna see that scoundrel is sent down the road?"

"I'll take care of Skipper as soon as I finish my coffee, Jack," the push said.

Ben was about to tell Pa that he had a bunch of syrup stuck in his hair, but he thought better of it when Pa stepped into the kitchen and pointed at the burned doughnuts. "You plan on goin' into the charcoal business?"

WINTER DREAMS

As Ben picked up the breakfast dishes, he thought back to the day Pa had asked him to the logging camp. That particular morning began like any other in Blackwater. Ben walked across town to the one-room schoolhouse, wishing he could skip his classes.

It was only the last week in October, but Ben was already sick of school. No matter how hard he tried to behave, he was always getting in trouble. He never sassed his teacher, Miss Stanish, or called her by her nickname, Miss Stench, like some of the boys did, but he was always getting scolded for blurting out answers and not being able to sit still. Ben couldn't help that he was talkative. He'd grown up chatting with Mrs. Wilson, a kindly, white-haired widow who'd helped raise him after his mother died. Ben was just a baby when he and Pa had moved into Evy Wilson's boardinghouse in Blackwater, and Mrs. Wilson had been like a grandma, mother, and aunt all rolled into one.

Mrs. Wilson was fond of saying, "Conversation is an

art worthy of cultivation," but in Miss Stanish's room a student wasn't allowed to say a word unless they were called on to stand beside their desk and recite.

When Ben forgot himself and spoke out of turn, Miss Stanish aimed her ruler at him like she was sighting down a rifle. "Benjamin J. Ward," she'd say. Her hair was pulled into such a tight bun that her eyebrows were half-moons. "Must I remind you to show proper decorum like your classmates?"

Ben wasn't sure what *decorum* meant, but he knew that the only other students in seventh grade were two prissy, apple-polishing girls named Abigail Montgomery and Martha Newcomb.

At exactly eight o'clock every morning, Miss Stanish rang her bell, and the nineteen first- through eighth-grade students lined up outside the front door of the school. With girls on the left and boys on the right, they marched silently in and hung their coats on opposite sides of the room.

Once the students took their seats, they had to keep their feet flat on the floor, backs straight, and hands folded on top of their desks. When Ben tugged at his itchy collar, Miss Stanish pointed her ruler and said, "Stop that fidgeting, Benjamin Ward."

After she took attendance, Miss Stanish said, "Class, you may stand and recite the Pledge of Allegiance." By then Ben was twisting in his seat and grateful for a chance to stretch.

The school day was a steady stream of reading,

spelling, arithmetic, and penmanship. As difficult as it was for Ben to sit in silence, it pained him more to watch the younger students forced to be so quiet. At recess Ben did his best to see that everyone had fun. King of the Hill was their favorite game, and Ben made sure that everyone got to play, even though Abigail and Martha teased him from the girls' side of the playground.

Ben didn't get yelled at again until after lunch, when Miss Stanish held her once-a-week Blab School session. During Blab School everyone opened their McGuffey readers and read out loud at the same time. It was hard enough for Ben to concentrate when it was quiet. His book was filled with dull poems by authors with yard-long names like William Cullen Bryant and Oliver Wendell Holmes. As soon as the chorus of readings began, he got an instant headache. Ben only moved his lips and pretended to read. But after a while he got bored and tried to improve on the seashell poem he was supposed to be studying:

> *THIS IS THE SHIP OF PEARL,*
> *WHICH, POETS FEIGN,*
> *SAILS THE UNSHADOWED MAIN.*

Instead, he recited his own lines:

> *IF ONLY THIS SHIP*
> *WOULD GO DOWN THE DRAIN*
> *AND SPARE MY ACHING BRAIN.*

"Benjamin!" Miss Stanish suddenly shouted behind him. "How dare you defile the words of 'The Chambered Nautilus'?"

○ ○ ○

That afternoon Ben had to stay after school and wash the blackboards, fill the inkwells, and carry in firewood.

On his way home he met Nell, a lady with bright red hair who owned the fanciest saloon in town. Nell favored purple dresses and tall, feathered hats. "You look like you've had a rough day, Mr. Ward," she called, her raspy voice blaring through the open door. "Care to belly up to the bar?"

"No, thank you, ma'am." Ben blushed even though he knew she was teasing. Most of the joints on Main Street were tents and rough board shacks, but Nell's place had a player piano, a plateglass mirror, and a polished mahogany bar with a brass foot rail.

Nell's long ruffled skirts swished as she stepped outside. The wooden sidewalk echoed under her high buckled shoes. "Is that old Miss Stinker being mean to you again?" Nell laughed and tousled Ben's hair.

Ben looked across the muddy street to see if anyone had overheard. "She ain't been too bad," he said.

Nell smiled. "You're a crafty man, damning by faint praise like that."

"I'd better get home, ma'am. I promised to help Mrs. Wilson with her canning."

"She's lucky to have you," Nell said.

When Ben got to the boardinghouse, Mrs. Wilson was already packing her first jar of pickles. The kitchen smelled of warm vinegar and dill. "You're late," she said, wiping her forehead with the back of her hand. "By any chance did Miss Stanish keep you after school?"

"How'd you know?"

"Abigail stopped by and told me."

"That girl's always snitching on everybody," Ben said. Abigail Montgomery lived next door, and her mother, Maggie, was Mrs. Wilson's best friend.

"If you didn't get into trouble, you wouldn't have to worry about people tattling."

"I suppose."

"No supposing—it's the truth. Wash your hands so you can help me put up the rest of these dills."

"Are you gonna tell Pa?"

"Maybe if I put in a good word, he won't tan your hide when he gets home."

"You mean if he gets home."

"Don't talk that way. Your father's a hard worker and a good provider."

Ben couldn't argue with the fact that Pa worked hard. After cooking all winter in a logging camp, Pa piloted the wanigan, the floating cookshack that followed the loggers on their spring river drive. When he returned to the boardinghouse in June, Pa was almost like a stranger to Ben. In the summer and early fall Pa worked at a local sawmill.

Before Pa sat down to supper that night, he turned to Ben. "I hear you got into trouble at school." The two other boarders smiled.

"Ain't there no secrets in this town?" Ben couldn't believe the news had traveled out to the sawmill.

"Were you running off at the mouth again?"

Ben nodded.

"I've half a mind to take you with me to camp next week."

"Are you joshing?" Ben sat up.

"You ain't learnin' nothin' washin' blackboards."

Mrs. Wilson stepped back from the stove and turned toward Pa. "What about Ben finishing school?"

"I only got one grade to go," Ben said. "What's the difference if I quit this year or next?"

"And I could use a cookee," Pa said. "Twenty-five dollars a month is good money for a boy Ben's age."

"Twenty-five dollars for being a cook's helper! That'd be a whole lot better than getting splinters from an old school desk."

"You measure an education by more than money," Mrs. Wilson said.

"I know," Ben said. "But you've always told me that life experience is important, too. Just think of all I'd learn about the logging business. And I could be with Pa! Best of all, I'd be outta your hair, Mrs. Wilson. Wouldn't that be dandy if I wasn't bothering you all the time? You'd be able to—"

"Whoa there." Pa chuckled. "Take a breath."

Mrs. Wilson walked over from the stove and gave Ben a hug. "Don't you ever call yourself a bother, Ben Ward. Looking after you has been one of the joys of my life."

"Can I go, Pa?"

"You promise to be quiet in my cookshack?"

Ben smiled and nodded.

"It's settled, then."

◉ ◉ ◉

At dawn on the following Monday, Pa and Ben rode to the Blackwater Logging Camp on the tote teamster's wagon.

Mrs. Wilson had taken Ben aside the night before and said, "You send me a letter now and then, so I can keep up on you and your pa. And speaking of Jack—" She paused and touched Ben's shoulder. "Your father may not always show it, but he cares a whole lot about you. The trouble is, having lived through the war and the loss of your mother like he has, he's carrying the weight of the world on his shoulders." Mrs. Wilson looked sad, then forced a smile. "And if Jack gets too crabby, you remind him that he'll catch more flies with honey than vinegar."

The air was cold and foggy as Ben and Pa climbed onto the wagon seat. When the teamster clicked to his matched grays, the freight wagon lurched forward, and the load of food barrels and cooking utensils clanked together in back. A chill breeze blew down Ben's neck, and the damp smell of rotting ferns mingled with the fresh straw that lined the wagon box. The trees were bare except for the smoky gold of the tamarack needles and the patches of red oak leaves that stubbornly clung to their branches. The road, which was well graded at first, got rougher as the wagon turned east and headed into a spruce swamp.

"How far is it to the camp?" Ben asked, his teeth rattling as the wagon bounced over a rock and into a pothole. He squinted into the hazy pink sun that was trying to burn through the fog.

"'Bout thirty-five miles, ain't it?" Pa called to the teamster over the squeaky wagon springs.

"Yep," said the teamster, a short fellow who had his cap pulled down over his ears. He was even less talkative than Pa.

"The road's bumpy in spots," Pa said to Ben, "but that won't matter once the snow smooths her over and they can haul supplies in by sleigh."

"Are we the first wagon to use this road?" Ben watched a stump in the middle nearly scrape the wagon tongue. Freshly cut brush and unlimbed trees were piled on both sides of the trail.

"I'll bet you made lots of trips already," Pa said, turning to the driver, "ain't you?"

"Yep," the teamster said.

When they finally arrived at the logging camp, it was almost dark. Ben's jaw dropped. "Nothin's built yet, Pa," he said.

"Looks like the cookshack and clerk's office are near done," Pa said. "And them log piles"—he waved down to the clearing—"show where the bunkhouse, barn, and blacksmith's shop will go."

"But where is everybody?" Ben had expected to see a camp full of loggers and teamsters, but the only men in sight were the clerk and the wood butcher.

"Till later in November there'll only be a couple dozen fellows here building the camp and swamping the roads. The saw crews can't start until the roads and the landing are done."

"Do you put up new buildings every year?" Ben said. Bark chips and wood shavings were trampled into the mud, and the air smelled of pine pitch.

"If the timber is real thick, we can work out of the same site a couple years in a row. Otherwise, we start fresh every season."

"You shoulda been here on the day I hauled the cook range in," the teamster said, stringing together more words than he'd uttered all day and pointing his thumb toward the doorless cookshack. "That was a doozy."

"We'd better unload and get some supper ready," Pa said. "The boys'll be coming in from the woods before too long."

"Will I get to help the loggers out at the cut when they start felling trees?" Ben asked. He gazed toward a towering pine stand to the south. "I bet those big ones really crash when they go down."

"We'll see," Pa said, stepping through the doorway. "For now, you'd better fire up the stove the driver brung us."

GOSINTAS

Though working in the woods had been Ben's dream, he soon discovered that cooking, dish washing, carrying water and wood, and doing laundry occupied him from before dawn until after dark. In the slack moments when he might have had a chance to visit the cut, Pa had him mop the floors, fill and clean the kerosene lamps, and organize the supplies in the storeroom. At times Ben got so tired of his chores that he almost wished he'd stayed in school like Mrs. Wilson had wanted.

On the morning Skip was fired, the cleanup took Ben twice as long as normal. He asked Pa, "You figure on hiring another cookee?"

"That's up to the push," Pa said. "It don't matter to me. I fed fifty jacks myself at a camp on Bow String Lake back in ninety-two. The two of us should be able to handle this outfit."

Ben did some figuring in his head as he rinsed off the silverware. There were twenty lumberjacks in camp. Once the ice roads were ready for hauling, the push would be hiring another sixty men. "How many loaves of bread will we have to bake when the full crew gets here?" he asked.

"Two dozen should do it," Pa said.

"Every day?"

"It might take a few more when the teamsters hire on," Pa said. "Some of them boys are big eaters. Speaking of food . . . you'd better run our supply order over to the clerk's shack." He handed Ben a list. "We're low on just about everything."

Ben hung up his apron and headed out the door.

A raven called from the top of a dead birch at the far end of the clearing as Ben walked. The Blackwater Logging Camp was laid out in the shape of a rectangle. The cook-shack stood at the west end, while the clerk's office and bunkhouse lay along the north side. Directly opposite the bunkhouse was the filer's shack and blacksmith's shop. The horse barn stood at the far end, sixty or seventy yards away.

Ben hated talking to the lumber camp clerk, Wally Lofquist, because Wally always tried to show off how smart he was. The men called Wally the pencil pusher, and a day never passed without him bragging about how he'd graduated from the eighth grade.

"Morning," Ben said, "Pa asked me to—"

"Do you know your gosintas?" the pencil pusher asked.

Ben frowned. "My gosintas?"

"Is that all you can do, repeat things? Are you a lumberjack or a parrot?" Wally adjusted the wire-rimmed spectacles on his nose and stared at Ben.

Ben blinked at the glare off Wally's bald head. Ben felt like saying, Why can't you just take this order and leave me be for once? But he took a deep breath instead. "I'm sorry, but I haven't heard of a gosinta."

"Didn't you never go to school?" The pencil pusher tapped his finger on the wooden counter.

"I finished the sixth grade last spring."

"Then you must have learned your gosintas." Wally put his elbows on the open ledger book and glared at Ben. Everyone in camp had to tolerate the clerk because they were working to get a stake in his book. No one got paid until the pencil pusher signed his time slip.

Ben shrugged. "Is a gosinta some kind of bird?"

"It certainly is not." Wally made a pickle face. "I hope you pay better attention to the work in this here logging camp than you did at your schoolhouse. Anyone with a smidgin of an education knows how many times two gosinta four and three gosinta twelve and the like."

"Why, you mean division," Ben said.

"Don't get smart with me, boy."

Ben decided it would be a waste of time trying to explain that gosintas and division were the same thing. "Here's Pa's order," he said.

"Order? If you had an order, why didn't you give it to me? I can't be gabbing with every greenhorned gazebo who happens by. I got work to do."

Ben trotted back toward the cookshack, shaking his head. Ben had gotten used to the old-timers calling him greenhorn or gazebo, but the one thing he couldn't adjust to was their crabbiness. Ben had considered Pa a champion grouch until he met Wally Lofquist. Compared to the pencil pusher, Pa was as sweet as shoepack pie.

THE BULL COOK'S THEORIES

"**B**en Ward?" Pa was calling from the kitchen as he opened the door. "Where in tarnation are you?"

Pa had a habit of yelling for Ben to come without looking up from his work. "I'm here," Ben said, running the length of the cookshack.

"You gotta learn to relax, Jack," someone said from the bench beside the potbellied stove. Ben recognized the voice of the bull cook, Windy, who was also the camp's general maintenance man. After the loggers left for the day, he usually stopped by for a visit.

"And you gotta learn to mind your own business," Pa said. Then he turned to Ben. "What took you so long?"

"You know how the pencil pusher is," Ben said.

Windy nodded. "I never have seen a fellow so contrary as Lofquist." Since Windy was toothless, his words had a mushy sound to them.

"And who asked you?" Pa said.

Pa called Windy Mush Mouth or Noise Box and thought he kept Ben from his work. Windy had a white beard that hung to the middle of his chest, and his shirts were only half buttoned no matter how cold it got. Windy checked every building in camp at least twice each night to stoke up the stoves. He was also the camp alarm clock. Every morning at four he woke up Pa and the push. An hour later he rousted out the teamsters so they could get their horses ready. The rest of the loggers got up around five-thirty.

Pa didn't like Windy, but Ben looked forward to the bull cook's stories. Windy had been working in the woods since 1848, and he knew the history of pine logging from Maine to Minnesota. Though Windy had been injured in a loading accident and wasn't strong enough to work in the woods, the logging company took care of him, like all their old and injured workers, by assigning him easier jobs.

"I heard you were tardy getting up this morning, Benny Boy," Windy said.

"This boy had a bad case of blanket fever," Pa said.

"I stayed up late getting the dishes done," Ben said.

"There's never no excuse for loafing," Pa said. "You're paid to get up and get the grub on the table."

"Two new fellows signed on this morning," Windy said.

"Any teamsters or top loaders?" Ben asked. The men had been felling trees all month and skidding them to the sides of the roads, but Ben was waiting for the four-horse teams to start hauling logs to the river landing.

"The ice roads ain't ready for highball logging yet.

·These boys claim to be loaders, but they look like short stakers to me."

"What's a short staker?" Ben asked as he chopped an onion.

"A short staker works at a camp a few days and then disappears." Windy hooked his thumbs under his suspenders and assumed his storytelling pose. "He figures the grub is better and the trees are taller down the road. I once knew a fellow who was nicknamed Nineteen 'cause he pulled paychecks from nineteen different outfits in one winter. But the worst sort of short stakers are the wild geese."

"How come?"

"They show up on a Saturday too late to start work but just in time for supper. They get three free meals on Sunday and a hearty breakfast Monday morning, but when it's time to hike to the cut, they're nowhere to be found."

Ben dipped Windy a fresh cup of black tea—the jacks called it swamp water—out of the pot that was always brewing on top of the woodstove. "Much obliged," Windy said. Then he stared at Ben.

"Is something wrong?"

"I was just noticing how much you're favoring your pa these days. You've got the same square chin and green eyes, and now that you're filling out, if you parted your hair down the middle and grew a mustache, you could pass as Jack Ward's twin."

Ben saw Pa smile behind the counter.

The bull cook took a swig of tea without checking to see how hot it was, and Ben asked, "Ain't you afraid of burning yourself?"

"This ole mouth is so tough from gumming moose meat, I could chew hot coals." Windy ran his thumb and forefinger along his chin. "But come spring I'm getting me some store-bought teeth."

Ben smiled. Pa said that Windy had been planning to buy a set of false teeth for years, but he'd never followed through. "How do you know those new jacks ain't steady workers?" Ben asked.

"If you study men, you learn, Benny Boy," Windy said. Pa banged some dishes in the kitchen, and Ben got up to help. But Windy kept on talking. "Every jack that comes to the tall timber is either a hider or a seeker."

"Every one?" Ben asked from the counter.

"I pride myself on knowing what makes these jacks tick." Windy grinned, sunken-cheeked. "The seekers are looking to make their stake. They're tired of life in the city or on the farm, and they're hoping for adventure. But once they sign on as a road monkey and start shoveling road apples, their hopes fade fast."

"What about the hiders?" Ben asked.

"They're running from something." Windy took a swig of tea. "It might be a bad debt. It might be family trouble. Lots of fellows are even hiding from the law. I once worked at a camp that had three John Johnsons. A name like that is a clear signal you'd best not pry." Windy paused to rub his crippled right leg.

"For some it's women trouble," the bull cook went on. "Arno's a good example. He was engaged to a lady down in Kansas City, but he got cold feet on his wedding day and ran off. By the time he realized he'd made a mistake, he figured it was too late to turn back. He kept pushing north till he hit the Blackwater Valley, and he's been logging up here for twenty years."

"How could a lady ever get over being left at the altar?"

"I expect she never would," Windy said. "But it works the other way, too. A man who's jilted by a woman sometimes lands so hard that he takes off for parts unknown. Why, we got one jack here who—"

"Ben," Pa snapped, turning to him, "with all your gabbing, have you gone and forgot the dentist's breakfast?"

"Sorry, Pa," Ben said, wiping his hands on a towel. Ben was supposed to bring meals to the dentist, Charlie Harrigan. Charlie was called the dentist because he sharpened the teeth on the crosscut saws. He lived alone in a separate shack and stayed up late so he could get the saws ready before the jacks left for the cut in the morning.

As Ben put Charlie's breakfast together, he couldn't help wondering—was the dentist a hider or a seeker?

A Trip to the Dentist

"Good morning." Ben tapped on the rough plank door with one fist while he balanced Charlie's breakfast in his other hand.

"Door's open," Charlie called.

Ben stepped inside. Charlie was bent over his wooden saw vise with a file in his hand. Charlie was a thin fellow whose skin was so white and papery that you could see little veins underneath. Though his hair didn't have a trace of gray, his slumped shoulders made him look old. He had a scraggly brown beard, and like the pencil pusher, he wore wire-rimmed glasses. He looked through his glasses when he was sharpening a saw, but he peered over the top when he talked to people.

Windy claimed that the dentist hadn't taken a bath for twenty-five years, but he didn't seem any dirtier than the other loggers. The yellowed sleeves of his woolen underwear suggested that when his old suit wore out, he just put a new one on over the old one.

The dentist's board shack was the only building in camp other than the four-hole outhouse that wasn't built out of logs. Only twelve feet by twelve, it had double sky-lights in the roof and was crowded with files, hammers, saw gauges, and a rack of Tuttle and Champion crosscuts.

Ben expected Charlie to complain about his breakfast being late, but he only waved toward the table and said, "Leave the grub there."

Charlie had a funny accent, and he used strange words like *barmy* when he meant *crazy,* and *codswallop* when he meant *nonsense.*

Charlie kept filing on his saw as Ben pushed aside a set hammer to make room for the food tray on the work-bench. Ben glanced at the wall. A few of the jacks owned a copy of the *Police Gazette* or *Argosy* magazine, but the shelves above Charlie's bunk held three rows of books.

"Your library reminds me of Mrs. Wilson's."

Charlie kept filing.

"She's the widow lady that Pa and I live with. Mrs. Wilson's got at least a dozen books in her collection—ones like *Pilgrim's Progress* and *Robinson Crusoe.* And she owns three different bibles, including one that's wrote in German."

When Charlie wouldn't talk, Ben picked up the previous evening's dishes and asked, "You need anything more?"

"A little grub and a lot of misery whips." Charlie looked up at Ben. "Misery whips is what I call these cross-cut saws. They're all I need to keep me busy."

Just then Ben noticed a row of small photographs hanging beside the bookcase. "Who are the ladies?" he asked.

"Years ago I went through what I call my romantic

period. I fell in and out of love four times in two years." Charlie gave a short laugh.

"That face looks familiar." Ben studied the last picture.

"You really blither on, don't you," Charlie said, setting down his file and turning his attention to his food.

"Blither?"

"Means you talk too much."

Ben figured that was a hint for him to go. As he left, he wondered what could have caused Charlie to revolt against baths. Lots of the jacks didn't bother to wash during the winter logging season, but Ben had never heard of a fellow skipping his spring cleaning.

Outside, a light snow was falling, and the air smelled of pine needles. The snowflakes caught flecks of sunlight and sparkled as they floated onto the tar-paper roofs of the camp. The fresh snow would be welcomed by the skid men—the teamsters who dragged the logs to the roadsides.

○ ○ ○

As soon as Ben opened the door, Pa said, "About time. We gotta get our crusts rolled out, or we'll never have these pies baked by lunchtime."

Ben grabbed a rolling pin. For lunch they prepared seven pies, six loaves of bread, a pot of beans, and a kettle of stew. They also brewed fresh swamp water and warmed more logging berries.

While Pa worked the pie crust flat, Ben asked, "Why don't you ever talk about Mother?"

Pa stopped his rolling pin but kept his eyes down.

"Don't you miss her?" Ben said.

Pa's hands tightened on the rolling pin, but he didn't look up. "Of course I do," he said. "A day don't go by without me thinking about her."

"How'd she die?"

"I've told you all that before. She took sick."

"Was it sudden?"

"What's the difference?" Pa's voice hardened. "No amount of jawing can bring her back. You just tend to your work."

"I'm sorry, Pa," Ben said, "but I can't help wondering."

Pa checked his pocket watch. "After all this gabbing, we're gonna have to give her tar paper to get the lunch done on time."

Ben smiled. Give her tar paper was Pa's favorite expression.

A few minutes later Ben was sliding the first of the pie crusts into the oven. He stopped and made a face.

"Did you burn yourself?" Pa asked.

"I was just figuring," Ben replied, struggling with the ciphering in his head, "how many pies we'll have to make when all eighty men get here."

"Thirty should be close," Pa said.

"And think of all the stew and logging berries and beans that many fellows will eat," Ben said.

"Don't forget the hundreds of cookies and rolls and doughnuts," Pa said.

Ben barely had time to sleep as it was. What would happen when his workload increased fourfold?

"It's almost noon," Pa said. "Hitch up the swingdingle."

"You want me to drive the lunch sleigh?"

"With Skip gone, somebody's got to haul this food to the cut."

"But I've never done it before."

"Do you know which end of the horse to point down the trail?"

"Of course."

"Then go see the barn boss and harness up Old Dan."

NEEDLENOSE AND THE SWINGDINGLE

It was still snowing lightly when Ben stepped outside, and the air smelled clean. The roofs of the camp and the branches of the balsams behind the barn were white with new snow.

Ben was nervous about having to talk to the barn boss, Needlenose Jackson. Ben had seen hundreds of lumberjacks pass through Blackwater, but Mrs. Wilson made sure he didn't meet too many up close. Mrs. Wilson was extra cautious in watching over Ben because her own son, Clayton, had been killed in the Civil War when he was only sixteen. Mrs. Wilson had told Ben how Clayton had joined the Union Army without her permission and had been shot during a training exercise. After the war Mrs. Wilson and her husband had moved from Pennsylvania to Minnesota, trying to leave their sadness behind. But as she told Ben, "We found there wasn't a corner of the earth far enough away from Lancaster County for us to get shed of our grief."

When the jacks hit the saloons hard in the spring, Mrs. Wilson worried about Ben getting hurt. "You play in the yard today," she'd say. "Those streets are not safe for respectable folks."

Blackwater's 193 citizens supported twenty-six beer joints and one church. On his way home from Sunday school, Ben sometimes peeked into the saloons. Unlike Nell's establishment, the cheapest joints were shacks and ragged tents with planks laid across two barrels for a bar. They served the local moonshine, jack juice, which was rumored to make men blind. On still nights the voices of men on Main Street and the music from the player piano in Nell's carried all the way down the river to Mrs. Wilson's boardinghouse.

The warm scent of the barn brought Ben's mind back to camp. He was glad to see that Needlenose had already led Old Dan out of his stall and had started harnessing him. The barn boss was a short, heavyset fellow who'd been a teamster in his younger days. He had the longest nose Ben had even seen. It looked like it had been stuck on his face by mistake.

"Good morning," Ben said, trying not to look at that nose. Ben had seen Needlenose chew out a new jack the week before for staring. He'd pushed his face up to man and said, "What you gawking at?" The poor fellow had nearly swallowed his chaw of tobacco.

"You driving Danny Boy today?" Needlenose asked.

Ben nodded. "It's good we're getting some snow, eh?"

"That depends." Needlenose glared at Ben. Since Needlenose spent his days in the dark barn, his eyes had a squinty look.

"I thought we needed snow to help with the skidding." Ben did his best not to stare.

"I can see you got a lot to learn about lumbering." Needlenose spit out a chewed-up piece of straw. "A little snow helps the skidding horses, but too much bogs them down." Ben helped him with the last harness buckles. "And remember that we've got to run the water wagon every night to build up the roads. Snow can make it hard to ice the ruts."

Ben studied Old Dan. The big black Percheron was a gentle, swaybacked animal whose log-hauling days were well past. The only work he was up to was pulling the lunch sleigh and skidding firewood. Though Old Dan's coat was peppered with gray and his gait had slowed, his eyes were alert.

"Even if Danny Boy's twenty years old, he's a fine puller." Needlenose patted the horse's shoulder. "Ain't you?" The barn boss always spoke kindly to his horses.

Old Dan perked up his ears at Needlenose's attention, but when Ben walked closer to the horse, the big animal blinked as if to ask, Who are you and what have you done with Skip?

"Hey, boy," Ben said, speaking low and soft like he'd seen teamsters do. "You ready to haul the lunch to the cut?"

"Be careful with that lunch talk," Needlenose said. "This old hay burner might think it's time for me to chop his dinner."

"You cut up hay for him?"

"Twice a day. His teeth are so far gone, that's the only way he can handle his feed."

As Ben helped Needlenose slide Old Dan's bit into place, Ben asked, "How come his front teeth stick way out, while his back ones are only little points?"

"They're plumb wore out. At least he's got more ivories left than Windy." Needlenose laughed.

Ben bent down to pick up the reins, but before he could say giddyap, Old Dan started out the door. Ben's arms jerked forward, and he almost fell down. As Ben ran to catch up, Needlenose said, "Old Dan knows his job so well that he don't need *you*."

Old Dan stopped at the door of the cookshack on his own. Pa came out and helped Ben hitch on the sleigh-mounted lunch delivery wagon, called the swingdingle. Pa pulled out his pocket watch. "Looks like it's time to load her up."

Pa and Ben worked fast to keep the food warm. After carrying out the wooden box of dishes, they set the steaming stew kettle, bean pot, and logging berries behind Ben's seat. Then they loaded the warm bread and pies into the blanket-lined compartments and latched the doors tight.

"I see the boys have already got a fire goin' at the cut," Pa said, glancing at the smoke to the south.

"Old Dan looks like he knows the way," Ben said. The horse was lifting up his front foot and pawing the snow.

"You'd better get moving," Pa said. "Them jacks don't cotton to cold beans."

Remembering how Old Dan had bolted out of the

barn, Ben climbed onto the seat and made sure his boots were planted on the footrest before he reached for the reins. The minute Ben picked up the reins, Old Dan jerked the swingdingle forward. The iron-tipped runners of the sleigh were soon hissing down the ice road. For the past three weeks the water wagon crew had been hauling water from the river at night and building up the road. They also cut grooves for the sled runners with a bull rutter.

Piloting the swingdingle wasn't as glamorous as felling trees or driving a four-horse team, but Ben was excited to get away from the cookshack. Ben never seemed to be able to do his jobs well enough for Pa. The afternoon before, Ben had been peeling spuds for an hour, but when he stood up to stretch his back, Pa had said, "Are you lolly-gagging again?"

Being cooped up in the kitchen with Pa from dawn until dark was like going to school seven days a week without recess. At school, Ben could at least look forward to a break at lunchtime. Here, lunch just meant more work.

Old Dan pulled the sleigh at a steady trot as he rounded the first two corners and climbed a low hill. Enormous red and white pines stood on both sides of the trail. The snow-covered crowns of the trees were so tight together that the ground was still patched with tufts of dry ferns in places. The men had started logging the stand farthest from the river, and they were working their way back toward camp.

Ben checked his watch. It was quarter to twelve—he'd get to the cut right on time. But when Old Dan reached the base of a second, steeper hill, he stopped suddenly. Ben clicked and whistled, but the horse only shook his head. Ben made a smacking sound with his lips like he'd seen teamsters do. He called, "Giddyap," and "Go, boy," and he flicked the reins. But Old Dan stood stiff-legged, blowing clouds of steam into the clear air.

Ben turned and checked the sleigh. Lumberjacks endured cold and snow and long hours in the woods without complaint, but if the kettles cooled, they would be angry. Men sometimes walked off the job when lunch showed up late. If Old Dan didn't get moving, Ben was going to be in big trouble.

"Pull, Danny Boy," Ben begged. "Please pull." But the horse kept blowing. Ben climbed down and walked to the front of the rig. When he got far enough ahead for Old Dan to see him past his blinders, the horse turned his head the other away.

"Dan!" Ben said, but the horse refused to look at him.

Ben trudged back toward the sleigh. What could he do? He heard the steady thunk of axes somewhere beyond the hill. Maybe he should run ahead and get help? Just then Old Dan lifted his head and jerked the swingdingle forward. "Whoa, Dan!" Ben yelled, running after the sleigh. "Stop, boy!"

Ben tried to jump onto the back of the sleigh, but his boots slipped on a rut and he fell. By the time he got to his feet, Old Dan was halfway up the hill.

"Daaann . . . ," Ben yelled, chasing after the horse. But the fresh snow made it hard to run. When Ben reached the top of the hill, the swingdingle was already disappearing around the next curve. "Daaann!" he called.

Two curves later, he saw that the smoke plume of the lumberjacks' bonfire was only a short distance away. He ran even harder. The men would tease him for the rest of his life if the lunch wagon arrived without him.

Just then he heard "Timberrrr!" He looked up. The snow shook loose from the top of a giant white pine. The tree began to sway.

Ben dashed forward. The tree crackled, and the branches whooshed as they picked up speed. He was going to die! Smaller trees snapped like twigs under the weight of the falling pine. Just before the trunk hit the ground, something smacked Ben's shoulder and knocked him down. The last thing he felt was the ground trembling. Then everything went black.

👁 👁 👁

"Hey, cookee." The voice sounded far away. When Ben opened his eyes, the first thing he saw was Packy's red stocking hat. "You'd better stop laying down on the job," Packy said, grinning. "If these jacks ain't served lunch soon, they'll be limbing you instead of the pine."

Packy helped Ben to his feet, but Ben tipped backward. "Steady there," Packy said, holding Ben's arm tightly. "You okay?"

Ben nodded, trying to shake off the dizziness. His head was pounding worse than it had during Miss Stanish's Blab School.

The lunch sleigh was parked just ahead. When Ben looked back at the huge tree, he knew he was lucky that only a single branch had hit him. "She's a big one, no?" Packy said. "Got to be a hundred feet tall." Packy brushed the snow off Ben's cap and handed it to him. "The sawyers like to drop them near the road so they're easy to skid, but this lady was sky bound—standing so straight there was no lean—and she got away. We'll get six sticks out of that grand dame for sure." By sticks Packy meant sixteen-foot logs.

"I thought that tree was gonna kill me."

"We've never lost a cookee to a pine yet."

"Quit your yammering, Frenchy, and cart that boy over here," yelled a big sawyer called Swede. "He's got stew to ladle up."

Ben still felt unsteady as he walked toward the sleigh. Packy's partner, Jiggers, had blanketed Old Dan and gotten out his pail of oats. The jacks were already lined up with their plates in their hands. When the men started working a new section of timber, they cleared a lunch area next to the road and laid logs beside the fire for seats. A row of balsam treetops stuck in the snow formed a windbreak to the north.

The smoke from the fire blew into Ben's eyes as he filled the plates, and it made his head ache. Once the jacks sat down, they worked their spoons nonstop. Ben was amazed to see that the men ate even faster in the woods than they did back in the cookshack.

"If we don't get after our beans quick out here," Packy said as he chewed, "they freeze to our plates."

Jiggers nodded. "We got to shovel in enough grub to hold us till supper."

Steam rose off the shoulders of the jacks' wool coats as they leaned toward the smoky fire that made Ben squint and turn his head. The men set their horsehide mitts beside them on the log, and they used their devil's cups—tin cups without handles—filled with hot swamp water to keep their hands warm between the stew and the shoepack pie.

Swede was the only one who complained when he saw the tea. "Swamp water again!" he groaned. "Somebody's got to talk to that belly robber. There's no way a fellow can enjoy pie without blackjack."

"Swede's a coffee-drinking fool," Packy said. "How many cups did you drink to win that bet last winter?"

"Thirty-seven," Swede said. "That's why some of the guys calls me Guzzling Gus."

"You drank thirty-seven cups in one day?" Ben asked, wondering if his aching head was affecting his hearing.

"In one hour, cookee." Swede spit into the fire. "Would you stop yapping and dish up that pie!"

As Ben was serving the pie, Jiggers winked. "So Old Dan got away from you, eh?"

Ben nodded. He braced himself for the teasing.

"Somebody should have warned you. That hoss always stops at that hill back there. We all call it Old Dan's

Hill. He'll rest a bit and blow, but you'd best keep your seat 'cause he don't dawdle long."

"I found that out."

"You can run after him like you done," Jiggers went on, grinning, "but if you want that much exercise, you might as well pull the sleigh yourself."

"Like Jack the Horse," Packy said.

"Who was that?" Ben asked.

"Jack was a teamster who cared more for his animals than any man I've ever seen," Packy said. "One day a horse came up lame, and Jack took his place in the harness."

Jiggers stood up and smacked his mitts together. "Speaking of the harness, it's time for us to get back to work." They tossed their tin plates to Ben.

Only after Ben had piled the dishes back on the swingdingle did he touch his forehead and find a spot of blood. No wonder he felt dizzy. The notchers were already at work with their axes, and the thunk of the blades gave Ben a throbbing headache.

As he climbed back onto the swingdingle, Packy dragged a broken skidding chain out of the woods. "Would you drop this off at the iron burner's shop?" Packy called.

"I'll stop by Arno's on my way in," Ben said, wishing Packy wouldn't yell.

"Thanks, cookee," Packy boomed. He slapped Ben's shoulder and tossed the chain onto the sled with a clatter. "But if Old Dan stops to rest on any of the hills, remember to keep your seat. Ha, ha . . ."

THE IRON BURNER

Ben watched Old Dan closely on the way back to camp, but the horse trotted the whole way without a rest. That made sense, since the ice road ran mainly downhill. The slope meant the teamsters would be able to haul logs from the cut to the river with the least possible effort.

Ben parked the swingdingle in front of the workshop that the iron burner and wood butcher shared. Arno Edwards did his blacksmith work in the front, while the wood butcher hewed oak bunks and sled runners in the back. The wood butcher also fixed harnesses, and he repaired sleighs, water barrels, and anything else made of wood. Windy liked to say, "There ain't nothing in a logging camp—other than tar paper, of course—that can't be made outta wood, leather, or steel."

Holding Packy's chain in both hands, Ben stepped inside. The air smelled of green popple and coal smoke. Arno stood at the forge in a leather apron riddled with burn holes. He was cranking his bellows and watching a horseshoe turn white-hot.

Arno raised a soot-blackened hand. "How's the belly

robber's son?" His voice rumbled like a locomotive engine.

Ben held out the chain. "Packy asked if you could fix this broken link." Smithing tools hung beside the forge. Two broken hammers lay in the corner along with kegs of horseshoes that had spilled onto the floor. Rodding and flat iron leaned against the near wall, which was hung with a half-dozen singletrees and chains.

Arno ignored Ben's question. Instead, he pulled the horseshoe out of the fire with his tongs and stepped forward. Ben coughed as the iron burner held the glowing metal in front of his face. He dropped Packy's chain and stepped backward, bumping into a chest-high mandrel.

"Give me a dime and I'll lick it," Arno said. His teeth gleamed in the firelight. In the corner the wood butcher glanced up from his work and smiled.

The red-hot horseshoe was about to singe Ben's eyebrows. His head pounded as he fished a dime out of his pocket and dropped it into Arno's hand.

Arno looked at the coin; then he lifted the horseshoe toward his open mouth. Just when the hot iron was about to touch his tongue, he stopped. Setting the tongs on his anvil, he licked Ben's dime and stuffed it into his pocket. Then he threw back his head and laughed.

"You got him there, Arno." The wood butcher joined in the laughter.

"Hey," Ben said. "What about my dime?"

Arno set the horseshoe back in the coals and cranked his bellows. All he said was, "Tell Packy I'll have his link welded by suppertime."

When Ben parked the swingdingle in front of the cookshack, he remembered that he needed to bring the dentist his lunch. He trotted inside. "Can we warm up some lunch for Charlie?" he called to Pa.

Ben tried to hide the lump on his forehead, but Pa didn't even look up from his pot. "Bring in the stew kettle, and I'll heat a bowlful while you unload the sleigh," Pa said. "That dentist's tar paper is already flapping, and we'd best not rile him."

As Ben stepped back outside, he was thinking that Charlie didn't seem any crazier than the rest of the lumberjacks. He stopped and stared. The swingdingle was gone! He thought his eyes were playing tricks on him until he looked down the clearing. Old Dan had already pulled the lunch wagon halfway to the barn.

"What in the devil is taking you so long?" Pa called through the doorway. Then he stuck his head out and saw Old Dan. "Would you look at that?" Pa said. Ben was afraid Pa was going to chew him out, but he chuckled instead. "Skip used to unhook the swingdingle before he came inside. Old Dan figures it's time for his afternoon nap."

Ben hurried across the snowy clearing with his tray. As he knocked on Charlie's door, he braced himself for a complaint. But the dentist only waved for him to set the meal down.

The musty smell of Charlie's shack reminded Ben of Mrs. Wilson's attic, a place he'd often played on rainy days. A small chest at one end of the attic held a collection of Mrs. Wilson's son's handmade toys: a wooden top, a set of painted blocks, and a carved train with wobbly wooden wheels and tiny cars linked together with worn loops of string. On gray afternoons Ben pulled his train through an imaginary city built out of blocks.

Charlie noticed Ben's cut. "How did you crack your pate?"

When Ben frowned, Charlie said, "*Pate's* another word for *head*."

"I took a fall," Ben said.

"You'd better pack some snow on it. That'll bring the swelling down." Charlie looked up at the skylight. "You're late again."

"It's been crazy without Skip around."

"I can understand that. I worked bleeding hard when I was a youngster, too."

"Whereabouts did you grow up?" Ben asked.

"It's a place you've never heard of on England's northeast coast called Newcastle upon Tyne." Charlie clamped a tooth-set gauge on a misery whip. "They call it upon Tyne because the River Tyne flows through town. It's a tired old smoke-blackened place." Charlie took off his glasses and rubbed his eyes. "I left home when I was a little nipper—only eight years old."

"Did you move to America?"

"No, I went to Christ Church College in Oxford."

"How could you go to college when you were eight?"

"I was picked to join the Christ Church Boys' Choir."

Ben looked at Charlie's matted hair and beard. The dentist—a choirboy?

"My mum said that when I was a baby, I'd hum along

with her and my sister. She claimed I could sing before I could talk."

"Mrs. Wilson likes to sing in the kitchen."

"Mrs. Wilson?" Charlie asked.

"'Member the lady I told you about who helped raise me?"

"You're so chock-full of information, it's hard to remember half of what you say."

"She sings real fine when she cooks. Mainly hymns."

Ben wondered if his mother had sung to him. Since Pa never talked about her, all Ben knew was that his mother had been a pretty young schoolteacher who was courted by half the fellows in the county. Ben wasn't even sure what his mother looked like because the big, oval-framed wedding photograph of her and Pa had gotten stained by a leaky roof years ago. In the picture Pa was his usual self, but his mother's face was so smudged, it was like trying to make out a face floating underwater. The only clear things were her pearl necklace and the lace collar of her dress. At times he could see a glint in her eyes, but it faded if he tilted his head the wrong way.

"What sort of songs are your favorites?"

"I don't mind a hymn myself, but—" Charlie stopped. "Now you got me blithering on, too. If I don't get after my victuals, it'll be teatime."

"Teatime?" Ben asked.

"You ask more questions than a barrister." Charlie half smiled. "Back home we had regular teatime in the afternoon and high tea later on."

When Ben got back, Pa said, "Did you get lost? I've already heated your dishwater."

Windy, who was sipping a cup of swamp water, said, "What happened to your head, Benny Boy?"

Pa turned to Ben. "Did you hurt yourself?"

"It's nothing," Ben said.

Pa pushed Ben's hair back. Ben tried not to wince. "Looks like you got kicked by a horse," Pa said.

"I just bumped my head."

"Go see the pencil pusher and get some medicine."

"I'm fine, Pa." Not the crabby clerk again.

"Get over there."

When Ben opened the door of the clerk's shack, the pencil pusher frowned. "Ain't I seen you once today?"

"I need some liniment," Ben said.

"For a horse or a man?" Wally asked. "Didn't nobody ever teach you nothing? You can't be tossing a big word like *liniment* at a fellow without explaining yourself. You might mean horse liniment. You might mean bone liniment." The push, who was sitting at a table, grinned.

"I got a cut." Ben pointed to his forehead.

"Cut!" the pencil pusher said. "Then you don't need no liniment at all. You need salve." He pushed his glasses up on his nose and turned around. "Let me see here," he said, pointing his finger at shelves that were stocked with a variety of medicines and compounds. Colored glass bottles, tins, and jars were arranged in rows: HINKLEY'S BONE

44

LINIMENT (the label promised it was good for everyday aches and pains); CASCARA CANDY CATHARTIC (guaranteed to cure headache, lazy liver, bad blood, constipation, worms, and bad breath); DAVIS VEGETABLE PAIN KILLER; SYRUP OF FIGS; PRUNIA; JAMAICA GINGER; and CASTOR OIL.

When his finger pointed to MCCONNON'S CARBO-SEPTIC SALVE, he said, "There!" and snatched the jar off the shelf. He turned the page in his ledger book. "Should I charge it to your account or your pa's?" He touched the tip of his pencil to his tongue.

"Pa didn't say."

"We'll put it down for you, then." He wrote in Ben's name and *25 cents*. Now Ben had lost a healthy chunk of his wages.

As Ben was turning to leave, Wally said, "By the way, you got yourself a letter today."

"Thanks," Ben said.

The letter was from Mrs. Wilson. Ben opened it on the way back to the cookshack.

Dear Benjamin,
    I hope this letter finds you well.
    We are having a quiet fall here in Blackwater.
The only excitement of late happened last Tuesday
evening when a bull moose wandered into town.
The moose was minding his own business, but our
civic-minded mayor, Sam Perkins, got it into his
head to scare him away. When Sam shot his ten
gauge into the air, the moose turned and charged.

Sam leaped out of the way, and the moose crashed through the front door of Nell's saloon. Though all of the injuries were minor, they say the player piano is a total loss. (The moose escaped out the back door.)

My new helper, Harley, cut his foot while chopping firewood. He's a nice enough boy, but he's oh so clumsy. I urge him to be more cautious, but he seems to be accident-prone. He's spilled the stove ashes twice, and the way he's tripping all the time, I'm afraid he's liable to fall into the rain barrel and drown himself.

I miss your steady hand, Ben. I hope you are learning some new recipes that you can share with me when you get back to town.

Give my best to Jack—tell him not to be such a sourpuss—and don't forget to say your prayers.

God bless,

Mrs. E. Wilson

When Pa saw Ben reading the letter, he asked, "Is everything okay with Evy?"

"She says you should try not to be a sourpuss."

"You write back and tell Mrs. Know-it-all Wilson that if I got any sweeter, I'd melt in the rain."

"Sure, Pa." Ben laughed.

Ben also showed the letter to Charlie, who said, "Your Mrs. Wilson is a superb stylist."

"Really?"

"Not only does she know how to put words together," Charlie said, "but she also has an ironic sense of humor."

"She does?" Ben folded the letter, wondering why Charlie was so interested in Mrs. Wilson's stories.

The rest of the day went so fast that Ben felt like he was still chasing Old Dan and couldn't catch up. By the time he had dried the lunch dishes, it was time to start peeling spuds for supper. He didn't finish cleaning up from dinner until eight-thirty. "I never thought Skip did much around here," he said.

"That boy mighta wasted too much breath on flattery," Pa said, "but he did what I asked."

After the dinner dishes were done, Ben couldn't go to bed until he'd set the tables for breakfast. Each of the twenty place settings had to be lined up in perfect order on the long wooden tables. The tin plates and bowls were placed upside down along with a devil's cup, which he centered on top of the bowl. Ben had to take his time, for if anything was out of place, Pa made him fix it.

As late as it was when Ben finished, he sat down and wrote back to Mrs. Wilson. Though writing a letter wasn't as comforting as having a talk in her kitchen, it helped him feel less lonesome. He also wanted to share Charlie's compliment about her writing.

DISHES AND DEVIL'S CUPS

Ben felt like he'd barely laid his head on his flour sack pillow when he heard Windy step into the bunk room and say, "Daylight in the swamp," to Pa.

Pa looked into the upper bunk as he slipped on his pants. "It's time to sling some hash. We've got to step lively now that that scalawag Skip has been sent down the road."

Ben wanted to tell Pa that his head ached way too bad for him to even think about getting out of bed. He couldn't believe Pa didn't notice his bruise. He felt the knob on his forehead and dabbed on some salve. It had swelled up twice as big this morning.

"Let's get moving," Pa said as he tied on his apron. "If we can't take care of twenty jacks, how are we gonna keep up when we have a full crew? Eighty men means four hundred flapjacks every morning."

The whole time Ben worked on breakfast, he thought about how boring it was being stuck in the kitchen. Pa believed in working 365 days a year. He was fond of saying, "Holidays and vacations are just an excuse for laziness." Though Mrs. Wilson chided him for it, Pa even worked Sundays. "The good Lord was entitled to rest on Sunday, seeing as he created the earth," Pa said, "but there ain't no man that ever done something so special that he deserved every seventh day off."

The lump on Ben's forehead throbbed all day long. When he was driving the swingdingle, he was glad that Old Dan behaved himself and that the jacks only teased him a little about the previous day's "tree dodging" and "horse jockeying."

For dinner he carried in a bushel of spuds and a peck of rutabagas. Though he and Pa had shoveled the syrupy dirt out of the root cellar, the vegetables still had a sweet scent to them. Of all the meals, dinner took the most time. In addition to the main course, which was cold sliced meat, Ben had to peel two different kinds of vegetables. No matter how many times he washed his hands, the sharp, rooty smell of the rutabagas wouldn't go away.

Preparing the meat was simple. Pa pulled a hunk out of the keg, soaked off the brine and saltpeter, and sliced it. Each evening Pa also baked cakes or rolls or cookies. Baking had been Pa's specialty when he was an army cook. "When some outfits were on the march, they ate nothing but moldy hardtack and cold beans," he told Ben, "but my crew always set up a full field kitchen, and we baked our boys fresh bread."

Since molasses cookies were on the menu that day, Ben had to make another trip to the root cellar and fill a pitcher with molasses. On his way back to the cookshack he looked to the west. The sky had opened up except for a few thin clouds. They would be in for a clear, cold night—perfect weather for the water tank crew to work on the ice roads.

"You close the spigot?" Pa asked when Ben got back.

"Yes, sir."

When Pa called the men to supper, Swede was the first one in the door. "How's Lumpy?" he asked Ben. "You been attacked by any tree branches lately?"

Packy said, "I heard the boy is hiring out as a horse trainer."

"Take a seat and shut yer yaps, you post and pole," Pa said. Pa called Packy Fence Post and Swede Telegraph Pole because Swede was a foot taller than Packy. Pa was the only man in camp other than the push who had the courage to put Swede in his place.

Ben hustled to keep the platters filled during the meal. The colder the weather, the more the fellows ate. Six more sawyers and skid men had signed on that afternoon. Ben heard the push say the camp roster would be at fifty men by week's end. How many pounds of spuds would Ben have to peel then?

When Ben brought out the cookies, Packy grabbed one in each hand and downed them in a single bite. He didn't stop until he'd gobbled up a baker's dozen.

Jiggers said, "Don't you think it's bad luck eating thirteen cookies?"

"It might be," Packy said, pushing himself back from the table, "but twelve never do seem to fill me up. Besides, it's worse luck leaving the table hungry."

EARLY SNOW

The following morning Ben was hoping he'd get a chance to ask Charlie about his early days in England, but Pa started hollering for Ben to get back to the cookshack before he'd even knocked on the dentist's door.

They were so busy that Ben was looking forward to his ride out to the cut with lunch. The sun was shining and the sky was a brilliant blue when he went to hitch up Old Dan.

"'Member what I said?" Needlenose asked as Ben opened the barn door. "You 'member?" He planted his face in front of Ben.

Ben tried not to stare at that nose. "I can't exactly recall."

"Snow, you greenhorned gazebo! I was talking about how snow is not always a good thing."

"But it's not snowing."

"Get back out there and open your eyes." Needlenose brought his nose to within half an inch of Ben's.

Ben nearly tripped as he stepped outside and looked up. "All I can see is blue sky and a few clouds."

"Not that way!" Needlenose spun him around. "Over yonder."

Low on the horizon in the northwest a black wall of clouds was building. "A storm's coming?"

"You'll be lucky if you get your sleigh back before it hits."

◉ ◉ ◉

Needlenose's prediction didn't miss by much. Ben had just started soaking the lunch dishes when the flakes started falling. "Make sure you get that water good and hot," Pa said.

"I know," Ben said. It took lots of soap and scalding water to wash off the hunks of frozen food. After he rinsed the silverware, he dumped it in a clean white grain sack like Pa had taught him and shook the pieces partly dry. Then he finished off the utensils by setting them in an empty pan on the warm stove. Ben figured Pa was being too cautious about being clean. The lumberjacks were so tough that there wasn't a germ in all creation powerful enough to make them sick.

When the push stopped by the cookshack for his afternoon cup of blackjack, his lips were tight. "A storm's blowing in, Jack," he said. "Maybe we'll have to ask your boy to help us with the snowplow tonight."

Ben was proud that the push had thought of him until he saw Pa's grin. "That's a good one."

"I'll say." The push slapped his knee and joined Pa in

laughing. "You keep practicing with Old Dan, tadpole"—the push grinned at Ben—"and someday you'll be driving a real team."

"Old Dan ain't that easy to handle," Ben said.

"Sure, son. Well, I'd better make sure that the wood butcher and Needlenose have got the plow rigged."

A short while later Ben heard the jangle of chains. He looked out the door. Packy was pulling a V plow made out of two half-sawn pine logs joined by a cross brace. "Look, Pa," Ben said. "They've rigged a six-horse hitch."

"We had a three-day blow over at Northome one year, and it took sixteen horses to pull the plow. The drifts got higher than the eaves of the bunkhouse."

As Ben watched Packy's team disappear, he recalled the push's laughter. Someday I'll show them, he thought.

UNDER TAR PAPER AGAIN

Pa woke Ben a half hour early so he could start shoveling. Ben lit a lantern, put on his mackinaw and wool cap, and stepped outside. He was glad to see that the storm had left less than a foot of snow. After he finished clearing the steps and the path to the root cellar, he put out his lantern and stood for a minute in the predawn stillness. The air smelled of birch smoke and ice. White starlight glinted off the rooftops and the snow-draped trees. The unbroken blackness in the east told Ben that sunrise was still a long way off, but Pa was already banging his pots and pans inside the cookshack. "Ben Ward," he called, "it's time to get our oatmeal boiling in here."

New lumberjacks continued to arrive almost every day. Some of the fellows caught a ride to camp on the tote teamster's wagon, but most of them walked the thirty-two miles from Blackwater. Every jack carried a white grain sack known as a turkey. The neck of the sack and one corner were knotted with a length of rope to make a carrying strap. Each turkey held a suit of woolen underwear, a pair of wool socks, a razor and sharpening strop, a towel, and a red or blue handkerchief.

The lumberjacks all wore heavy wool caps, wool shirts, wool trousers, and rubber-soled boots. Their hands were protected by horsehide mitts and woolen liners. With the exception of Charlie, everyone started the season with new clothes.

Before lunch a fellow named Poultice Pete walked into the cookshack. Though most of the jacks were husky fellows, Pete was rail thin. "Make sure you keep downwind of him," Pa whispered to Ben.

"How come?"

"He sleeps with a poultice of turpentine and onions plastered across his chest."

"Howdy, Pete," Windy said. "Looks like you ain't even worn out the creases in that shirt yet."

"I like to start out fresh in a new camp," Pete said. "Why bother to patch up clothes when it's easier to toss the old ones out? Besides, I travel so light that a needle and thread would weigh down my turkey."

"Skinny as you are, you can't travel no way but light," Windy said. "Didn't those farmers feed you nothing out in Dakota? A strong wind would blow you back to the prairie."

"We'll fatten him up," Pa said. "The boys used to say Poultice was so thin that it took him ten minutes to cast his shadow."

Ben was amazed at how happy the men were when they arrived at camp. Before Pete left the cookshack, he said, "It sure feels good to be under tar paper again. These woods is heaven after a dusty summer of threshing grain. Ain't nothing sweeter than taking a big drink of Minnesota pine air and having fresh tar paper over my head."

Windy grinned at Ben. "Didn't I tell you that tar paper is the main ingredient of a lumber camp?"

Ben nodded as Windy took a sip of swamp water. "This place is a lot fancier than the State of Maine camp I worked in when I was your age. A dozen of us slept under one big blanket. Only way we could keep warm was to bring the oxen inside at night. And every meal was the same—a bean pot cooked over an open fire."

"Wasn't it dirty living with animals?" Ben asked.

"I'd rather bunk with oxen than some of these jacks."

"But your bunkhouse is clean," Ben said.

"You wait until the smell of that new tar paper wears off. We'll hatch out every breed of bug you can imagine. Our lice crop is getting healthier every day. It's the fault of them jacks."

"For not washing?" Ben asked.

"Of course they don't wash, but that's not the main problem," Windy said. "I always tell the fellows not to kill them lice, but they keep swatting 'em."

"What's wrong with that?" Ben asked.

"Why, ain't you heard? If you kill one, a hundred more come to the funeral." Windy laughed, his toothless mouth wide open, and slapped his knee.

"I sure do wish I had me some sound choppers." He rubbed his jaw. "When I get my store-bought teeth, I'm gonna bite off a hunk of beefsteak and chew and chew."

"Speaking of chewing," Pa said, tossing Ben a stirring spoon, "If we don't give her tar paper—"

Ben finished for him: "These jacks won't be getting no lunch."

THE PHOTOGRAPH

After a week without Skip, Ben was dead tired. On Sunday he asked Pa, "Since the push has added so many men, you suppose he'd hire us a cookee?"

"Let me know if you can't hold up your end." Pa spooned some baking powder into a mixing bowl.

"I don't mean that I can't do the work."

"Either a fellow can do a job or he can't." Pa banged the baking powder can on the counter to break a clump loose. "And if you ever get to the can't stage, just let me know." He shoved the spoon in hard.

Why did Pa hate questions so much? From the time Ben was little, Mrs. Wilson had always encouraged him to ask how and why things happened, but Pa was more inclined to say, "Curiosity killed the cat."

When it came time to deliver Charlie's breakfast, Ben blurted out something he'd been itching to ask:

"Is it true you haven't taken a bath for twenty-five years?"

Charlie looked up from his misery whip. His eyes narrowed. Ben stepped back. His mouth had gotten him in trouble once again.

Then Charlie smiled. "Those blinking jacks do love to exaggerate. As a matter of fact, it's been sixteen years and"—he paused—"three months."

"That's longer than I've been alive."

"I imagine it is." Charlie turned back to filing the raker teeth.

"So who is that lady?" Ben pointed to the last of the four photographs hanging beside the bookshelf.

Charlie studied the angle of his file. "There's some things in life a man tries to forget."

"It was wrong of me to pry," Ben said.

"As a matter of fact," Charlie said, "that picture is one reason why I turned against bathtubs."

Ben studied the photograph. The young woman's black curls were combed to one side. Though her mouth was small and serious, her dark eyes seemed to be laughing at something. Those eyes felt familiar.

"I met Miss Lucinda on the first day I arrived in Grand Rapids." Charlie set down his file. "I was at the depot waiting to change trains. I had a one-way ticket to a town called Pembina. That morning I'd asked the stationmaster in Duluth what place in Minnesota was the farthest from everywhere.

"Since I had time to kill in Grand Rapids, I walked

down to the bank of the Mississippi. I'll never forget how bright and blue that day was. After a winter of coal smoke and fog in England, I kept admiring the sky."

"But why'd you ever leave England after your fancy Oxford education?"

"It was all on account of a lady."

Ben looked back at the photograph.

"No, not her," Charlie said. "She enters the picture later."

"Bennn . . ."

Ben stuck his head out the door.

Pa stood on the cookshack steps. "You know your holiday don't start until after we get things cleaned up."

"Sorry, Pa."

"He sounds bollocking mad. Best get moving," Charlie said.

Though Pa's idea of a holiday wasn't much, he did allow Ben a couple of free hours on Sunday afternoons. The day began with Pa and Ben cooking breakfast and lunch, but for supper, along with the usual beans and logging berries, they served only cold cuts, fried spuds, and bread left over from their morning baking.

Sunday was also the day that a few of the jacks went to the boiling-up shack behind the bunkhouse to take a bath and wash out their socks and underwear. They filled a washtub with water warmed on a barrel stove and used a wooden paddle to swish their clothes around. After they hung their clothes above the stove, they used the leftover wash water for bathing. Once a week Ben had to go to the boiling-up shack and wash out all the aprons and towels, and Pa insisted that he and Ben both take baths.

After Ben finished the lunch dishes, he walked down to the bunkhouse to watch the fellows tease each other and arm wrestle and swap stories.

The bunkhouse was a narrow log building with double bunks lining both walls. Though the top bunks were warmer, the fellows up there had to be careful they didn't rap their heads on the ceiling when they climbed in and out of bed.

When Ben opened the door, he was surprised at the quiet. Normally someone shouted, "Hey, cookee," or yelled about the draft. But everyone was clustered around the stove in the middle of the room. Windy had his watch open.

Ben climbed onto a deacon's bench for a better view. Packy had his bare feet on a chair, and he was sitting on top of the woodstove!

"What's goin' on?" Ben whispered to Windy.

Windy kept his eyes on his watch. "A stove-sitting contest."

Beads of sweat were running down Packy's forehead. Ben could smell burning wool. "He's close to the record," Windy said.

Packy shifted his feet on the chair, and Swede shouted, "No fidgeting allowed!"

"I ain't moving," Packy said. But a moment later he jumped up and danced around the room, fanning the back of his pants.

The fellows hooted and hollered.

"What's his time?" Arno said.

"One minute"—Windy studied his watch—"and forty-six seconds."

Arno slapped Packy on the back. "That makes you the winner by"—Arno subtracted in his head—"six seconds."

"I say he fidgeted," Swede said.

"You're a sore loser." Packy grinned.

Swede looked at Ben. "How about you, cookee? You're used to a hot kitchen. I bet you'd be a grand stove sitter. Come on," he said, grabbing Ben's wrist with his huge hand. "How'll you know unless you try?"

"I'd rather not," Ben said.

Swede was about to boost Ben up onto the stove when Windy said, "That's the boy's choice, Swede."

Ben was surprised at how fast Swede stopped. Though Windy wasn't as strict as Pa, he was the boss of the bunkhouse. The jacks knew that if they got on his bad side, they'd end up sleeping in the north corner, where snow sifted between the chinking.

Once Windy assigned a fellow a bunk, he couldn't move without permission. A man's bunk, along with half the deacon's bench beneath it, was his private territory. If a jack so much as set his cap on another fellow's bunk, a fight could break out, and it was Windy's job to make sure that didn't happen.

After Packy's pants cooled down, he picked up an ax and walked over to the grinding wheel. "How's that lump on your head, cookee?" he said as he pumped the big stone wheel with one bare foot.

"The swelling's down."

"You're lucky it was only a branch that hit you."

"I'll say," added Jiggers, who was whittling by the stove. "That pine coulda flattened you to a flapjack."

When Packy finished, he held the ax up for Ben. Packy prided himself on being a master axman, and he liked giving Ben tips on how to sharpen a blade and hang the ax, meaning how to fit the handle to the owner. "How's that for an edge?" Packy asked. The steel gleamed in the light from the skylight vent. He pulled a wooden match out of his pocket and shaved off slivers, counting, "One, two, three, four," as the shavings curled and fell.

Swede, who'd taken a seat at the card table, said, "That cookee has got way too much talent to waste his time ax-sharpening. He should become a jockey and train Old Dan. The two of them would be a terror on a racecourse." Ben had to smile at the thought of himself riding a one-ton draft horse down a racetrack.

Windy said, "When I first saw that bump on your head, I thought maybe an agropelter had cracked you."

"What's an agropelter?" Ben asked.

"You know what a widow maker is, don't you?"

Ben nodded. Everyone knew about widow makers—dead branches that fell out of trees and killed or injured loggers.

"Most folks think that when a branch hits a jack over the head, it's caused by the wind or an ax shaking it loose. But that ain't always the case. There's a critter called the agropelter that lives in these woods. Most of the time when a jack's killed by a stray limb, a 'pelter's to blame."

"Why haven't I ever seen one?" Ben asked.

"They're real secretive. They live in hollow trees and feed mainly on hoot owls and woodpeckers. The only fellow I know who sighted one was Ole Pedersen. I was working with Ole off the Rat Tooth Trail in the fall of 1889. He was walking back from the cut when a branch knocked him flat."

"How'd he know an agropelter done it?" Jiggers interrupted.

"I'll get to that, if you'll hold your breath long enough for me to finish," Packy said. "Luckily, the branch that critter flung at him was rotten, and it shattered on top of his head. Ole was groggy, but he looked up in time to see an agropelter leaping through the treetops like a wild monkey. He said the critter was an ape-faced animal with big muscles and hairy, six-foot-long arms. Those arms helped him swing through the trees so fast that he was just a blur. That's why none of us have ever seen one. Ole figured that 'pelter was strong enough to hit a jack's cap at fifty paces."

Ben smiled at the tall tale. But as the men turned back to their card game and the north wind howled over the stovepipe, he couldn't help wondering if there might be a hint of truth in Packy's story. With the miles of wild timber in the north, who was to say what sort of creature might be lurking beyond the reach of the tote roads?

NEVERS AND THE SISSY STICKS

As more loggers hired on, the Blackwater Logging Camp shifted into high gear. The cooking was taking Pa and Ben longer every day. But whenever the push asked Pa if he needed help, he said, "Me and Ben are doin' fine."

Ben felt like blurting out, "What about sleep, Pa? How am I gonna get breakfast on the table when the time comes that I'm still doin' the dinner dishes at daybreak?"

Things were so hectic that Ben never had a chance to listen to Windy's stories. And whenever Ben took Charlie his meals, he had to hustle right back to the cookshack.

Luckily the push took it on himself to bring a cookee over one afternoon. "This boy stopped by looking for work, Jack," the push said. "Since he's got cooking experience, I wondered if you wanted to try him out?"

Before Pa could answer, Ben said, "An extra hand wouldn't hurt, Pa." Then he crossed both fingers behind his back.

Pa looked ready to snap at Ben, but he turned to the boy and asked, "How'd you get fired from your last job?"

"I didn't get fired, sir." The boy drawled out *fired* so it sounded like *fard*. "I quit."

"Who'd you work for?"

"Matt Maki."

"He's a good cook."

"I know, sir," the boy said. "But I got tard of eatin' fish soup and boiled taters."

"Matt does favor fish stew. What's your name?"

"Nathaniel Evers."

"Well, Nathaniel, we fry most of our spuds around here."

"I'd like that, sir."

"What do you say, Pa?" Ben asked, his fingers still crossed. Nathaniel was a short, skinny boy with thin blond hair and a chin that came to a sharp point. He shifted his weight from one foot to the other as he waited for Pa to answer.

"You're a mite scrawny, but I suppose we could give you a chance. Let's see what kind of potato peeler you are." Pa tossed him a paring knife. "But I figure Nathaniel Evers is way too long a name for a toothpick like you. I say we make it Nevers."

"I reckon I bin called worse," Nevers said, reaching for a potato and stepping up to the counter.

Nevers grinned as the peelings started to fly. "What are you laughing at?" Pa asked.

"I ain't laughin', sir." Nevers drew out his words long and slow. "That's my natural look."

Ben started peeling, too. He was amazed at Nevers's

hands. "Where'd you learn to peel spuds so fast?" Ben asked as a wet potato squirted out of his grip and rolled onto the floor.

Still grinning, Nevers bent down and tossed the potato back to Ben. "If I wanted to eat, I had to work."

"Didn't your parents feed you?" Ben scratched his cheek with the back of his hand.

"My mama died of a flu epidemic down in South Carolina two years ago, and the county put me in an orphanage."

"I'm sorry to hear that. Did your pa die, too?"

"I don't rightly know where he's at. A few years back Daddy give up on tenant farming and went to work in a cotton mill." Though Nevers talked slowly and deliberately, his fingers rotated the potato so fast that it blurred. "Mama warned Daddy those mill towns was fast places, but he wouldn't listen. At first he strutted home all proud and give us some money. Then one Saturday he didn't come home." Nevers tossed the peeled potato into the pan and started on another one. "We never saw him again.

"After my mama died, I was sent to the orphans' home, but I run off. They brung me back three times, but the fourth time I kept on goin'. I'da ruther joined Mama in the cemetery than stay in that sorry place."

"How old were you?" Pa asked from the far end of the counter. Since Pa wasn't a good listener, Ben was surprised that he was paying attention to Nevers's story.

"Eleven and a half."

"And you hiked all the way to Minnesota?" Pa asked.

"I have to admit it warn't easy," Nevers said. "I'm so little that every cop figured I was a runaway. The only way I got through was by hidin' out near the railroad yards and ridin' the freights. I panhandled a few crumbs of food and warmed myself by stealin' kerosene out of brakemen's lanterns—a sand-filled pail makes a tolerable hand warmer on a winter night. My closest call came in Duluth. I'd just got caught borrowin' a shirt off a clothesline, and a cop was set to haul me in. But an old jack walked up and said, 'This boy's with me.' Next thing I knew, I was on the train to Cusson. That same jack talked a clerk into signin' me on at the Ash Lake Loggin' Camp."

"You've done good by yourself," Pa said. "Losing one parent is rough on a youngster, but losing both would test his mettle."

"Ben's lucky to have his family," Nevers said.

"All I got is Pa," Ben said. "My ma passed away, too."

"That's a shame," Nevers said.

"We miss her a lot," Pa said, scraping the side of his mixing bowl. Ben was hoping Pa would say more, but he looked at the half-filled pan of spuds instead and said, "You boys better give her tar paper if we're gonna get supper on the table before next week."

After hearing Nevers's story, Ben realized that his own life had been pretty easy. Pa and Mrs. Wilson expected him to work hard, but they'd always done their best to take care of him.

The boys were just starting on the carrots when Windy stopped by. "How's our new cookee?"

"I'm fine." Nevers kept working on a carrot as he studied the bull cook. Ben noticed that Nevers's feet shifted nervously whenever he met someone new, like he was getting ready to run.

"That's good," Windy said. "These boys have been shorthanded since their last cookee decided to give Jack a syrup bath."

"Nevers is a fine potato peeler," Ben said.

Windy nodded. "I don't doubt that." Then he looked Nevers in the eye. "You don't smoke, do you, boy?"

"Why you askin'?"

"I advise you to lay off the cigs at this camp. The two things the push—Collins is his name—hates more than anything else in this world are cigarettes and thermometers. He tolerates chewing tobacco and pipes, but he calls cigarettes sissy sticks. If he catches a man smoking, he fires him on the spot."

"Don't he warn 'em?" Nevers asked.

"He figures fellows should be smart enough to know that much on their own. But the push has got such a soft heart that he won't send a man down the road by his lone self. He waits till he catches two of them sissy-stick puffers, and he fires them both at once. That way they can keep each other company on the way home."

"But why does he hate thermometers?" Nevers asked.

Ben said, "The push claims if the fellows know how cold it is, they won't want to work. He only allows one thermometer in camp, and keeps it to himself."

"That's right," Windy said. "The push never works the

horses when it's colder than forty below. That can kill 'em, you know. But the men have to go out up to fifty below."

"Isn't he afraid of killing the men?" Nevers asked.

Windy laughed. "I never saw a lumberjack die of the cold as long as he kept moving."

Pa picked up the vegetable pan and said, "Nevers has got the quickest fingers with a paring knife I've ever seen."

"It helps that my hands are small, sir," Nevers said.

"And you're polite, too," Pa said. "I like a cookee who ain't always asking a bushel basket full of questions."

When it came time to serve supper, Nevers worked twice as quickly as Skip had. As he ladled up the beans with one hand and passed a loaf of bread with the other, Pa said, "I can see that you're one boy who don't let grass grow under his feet."

"I ain't never been accused of dillydallying, sir."

During the cleanup Nevers proved that he was a speedy dishwasher, too. But the thing that impressed Ben most was how quickly he set out the breakfast dishes. Nevers walked alongside the tables, plunking down each plate and centering a bowl and cup on top without breaking his stride.

By the time they'd finished the tables, Ben was tuckered out. But Nevers was still grinning. "Don't you ever get sick of doing kitchen work?" Ben asked.

"I'm used to being as busy as a stump-tailed cow in fly time. Besides, your pa's easy to work for."

"But Pa is always ornery."

"If you think he's ornery, you ain't seen many lumber camp cooks."

Ben looked doubtful.

"It's true. Before I hired on with that Finn cook Maki, I worked for an old coot named Sorghum Sam. Got his nickname 'cause he flavored everything with sorghum and molasses. The only thing worse than his cookin' was his temper. One day a green jack asked why the stew was so sweet. Without saying a word, Sam picked up the whole kettle and threw it at the door. The hinges busted, and carrots and spuds and moose meat flew all over. That jack never spoke in the cookshack for the rest of the winter."

The whole time Ben and Nevers were getting ready for bed, Nevers kept telling one funny story after another. Pa normally liked it quiet before bedtime, but he got a chuckle when Nevers told about a mean fellow in Ohio who'd hired him to dig a drainage ditch. "I worked three days," Nevers said, "but instead of paying me like he promised, that good-for-nothing trash run me off with his shotgun. I got even by sneaking back that night and shoveling the ditch full again."

Once his story was done, Nevers fell asleep as quickly as he set tables. One minute he was jabbering full speed ahead. The next minute he was snoring like he'd been cracked with a brickbat.

Pa was soon rattling the rafters, too. Ben lay for a long time trying to sort through his first afternoon with the slow-talking Carolina boy who never stood still. Skip had been mean and sneaky right from the start. Working with Nevers felt like it was going to be interesting, but more complicated.

THE HOSPITAL FUND

Though the lumberjacks were normally slow to accept a newcomer, the men took an immediate liking to Nevers. Even the plodding iron burner, Arno, was impressed with Nevers's serving speed at breakfast. "I used ta be able to empty a platter of flapjacks before a cookee could begin to fill it," Arno said. "But ain't no way I can put 'em down as fast as that Nevers can pile 'em up."

"He must be greasing his boot heels to move that quick," Packy agreed.

Later that morning as they were making pie crusts, Pa held up Nevers's pie tin before he put it in the oven and said, "That's about the finest fluted edge I've ever seen." Ben looked at his own tin, wondering what was wrong with his crust.

Ben was ready to wish for Skip's return when Nevers finally showed he was human. As Ben and Nevers were picking up the baking pans, Nevers accidentally tipped over the garbage pail, and he let out a choice cuss word.

Pa glared at Nevers. "What did you say?"

Nevers repeated the word, and Pa said, "That'll cost you."

"Cost me what?"

"See that kitty over there?" Pa pointed to a coffee can labeled HOSPITAL FUND next to the door. "You got to put a penny in that can every time you cuss in my shack."

"Don't I at least get a warning?"

"Nope."

In the middle of the morning Pa came back from the clerk's office with a letter. "Evy Wilson's writing to you again." Pa handed the envelope to Ben.

"It's from our landlady," Ben explained as he broke the wax seal and opened the letter.

Nevers admired the perfect script of the address on the envelope: MASTER BENJAMIN J. WARD, BLACKWATER LOGGING CAMP. "That penmanship is fine enough for Mrs. Wilson to author herself a handwriting book," Nevers said.

"She prides herself on being neat. Her needlework is the same way—you'd think every stitch was done by a machine."

"So what did she say this time?" Pa asked.

Ben skimmed through the letter and smiled.

"Is it funny?" Nevers asked.

"In a way," Ben said. "Mrs. Wilson is a sweet church-going lady who'd never harm a soul, but she fixes on gore sometimes."

"Like blood and guts?"

"And death and dying," Ben said. "We had a man west of town fall in front of a hay rake last summer, and she wasn't content until she'd heard all the gruesome details."

"Let's hear it, then."

"First I should explain that Mrs. Wilson's closest friend is her neighbor, Maggie Montgomery, the preacher's wife. She's one of the few ladies in town who isn't a saloon gal."

"Get on with it," Nevers said.

Dear Benjamin,

    Thank you so much for your letter. You be careful of that nasty horse, Dan, and don't let him run away from you again. Speaking of livestock, I read in the paper that the champion guernsey cow from Grand Rapids that we saw at the fair last summer fell and broke her hip. It's a pity that the owner had to put such a lovely creature down.

    Blackwater has been quiet now that most of the jacks are working in the woods like you and your pa. But we do have a few fellows passing through town. Sadly, a certain disreputable saloon owner—you know his name as well as I do—is still knocking jacks over the head and stealing their money. Bodies are turning up weekly. I certainly wish the authorities would do something.

    On Sunday morning poor Maggie Montgomery got the scare of her life when she discovered a corpse behind the church. She was carrying a bottle of communion wine, which she promptly dropped and broke. The dead man was lying right on the back steps and was bludgeoned so badly that positive identification was impossible. We all suspect the aforementioned bartender.

Give my regards to your father, and remember your prayers.

God bless,

Mrs. E. Wilson

P.S. Tell Mr. Charles Harrigan that if I want a literary analysis of my letters, I'll request one.

"Is *bludgeoned* being hit over the head?" Nevers asked.

"The same," Ben said as he refolded the letter.

"I can see where Mrs. Wilson likes her gore. We had a neighbor like that back home—Sally Hinricks. She was nice as pie, but nothing perked her interest more than hearing about a man falling into a vat at the tannery, or a two-headed calf being born."

As Ben folded the letter to put it back into the envelope, he saw that Nevers looked like he wanted to ask him a question.

"You can read it again if you like," Ben said.

"It's your letter."

"I don't mind." Ben handed the page to Nevers.

"I can't read."

"What?"

"None of the menfolk in my family can read. We were

too busy farming to bother with school. I wasn't lucky like you."

"You call going to school lucky?" Ben asked.

"It's better than pickin' boll weevils offa cotton plants."

"Didn't you at least learn to read hymns in church?"

"Our congregation couldn't afford hymnbooks," Nevers said, "so our minister just sang the verses and we repeated them back."

Ben had never once thought of going to school as being lucky, but he couldn't imagine not being able to read a letter or follow along in a hymnbook.

At lunchtime Ben found out that Nevers had another weakness. It happened when Pa asked Nevers to bring the lunch tray over to the dentist's shack.

Ben and Pa were loading the swingdingle when Nevers came back. "Are you feeling poorly?" Pa asked Nevers. "You look a little green around the gills."

"I get a queasy stomach sometimes, sir. And I can't stand the smell of Charlie's ole shack."

"You'll get used to it," Pa said.

"I don't think so, if you'll pardon my back talk. It reminds me of the closed-up smell of the orphanage. They wouldn't never open the windows. Didn't matter if it got hot enough to melt candle wax."

Instead of hollering at Nevers for complaining, Pa said, "If the stink bothers you, I reckon there's other jobs around here."

Ben didn't mind delivering Charlie's lunch, but how

come Pa had let Nevers off so easy? If Ben complained about a job, Pa made sure that he did it twice as often.

Ben took his letter along when he went to pick up the lunch tray. Charlie would enjoy reading Mrs. Wilson's news.

HIGHBALL LOGGING

As the hauling season drew closer, the energy in the camp rose. By night the water tank crew kept building up the ice roads. By day the sawyers kept felling pine. Back in camp Arno checked the calk shoes on the horses, and the wood butcher worked extra hours finishing the twin-bunk oak sleds that had to be strong enough to haul a hundred tons of wood.

Ben thought the new cookee might slow down after his first few days, but Nevers was forever drumming his fingers on a table or tapping his boot on the floor.

"You got ants in your pants, boy?" Pa asked him three or four times a day.

No matter how fast Nevers worked, his swearing was getting him on Pa's bad side. A cup of flour tipping off the counter or a spatter of grease hitting his arm was all it took to get the cuss words flying.

At first Pa pointed to the kitty every time a swear word popped out, but after a while Nevers got so used to paying up that he walked over to the coffee can on his own and plunked in a penny. One afternoon Nevers even had to pay double when he caught his apron on the oven door, swore, and then cussed himself out for not being able to stop his cussing!

"Maybe you should try to use a regular word in place of the bad ones," Ben said.

"Like what?" Nevers tapped the toe of his boot on the floor.

"Instead of cussing, why don't you just say *Shoot* or *H-E-double toothpicks* or *Petunias*?"

"I gotta try something," Nevers said, "or I might as well sign my whole paycheck over to the hospital fund."

Ben's plan worked at first. "Thanks, Ben," Nevers would say, grinning each time he held himself in check. Then just before supper Nevers brushed his forearm against the stovepipe. He jerked back and swore a blue streak as he ran to the water pail and plunged in his arm.

"Boy, you could make a sailor blush with that tongue of yours." Pa shook his head as he rubbed some lard on Nevers's burn. "I counted a good nickel's worth that time."

Nevers lifted his arm carefully. "Would you settle for three cents?"

◉ ◉ ◉

The good thing about Nevers's foul mouth was that Pa had less time to holler at Ben. It was also entertaining. Nevers had a true gift for cussing, the likes of which Ben had never seen. While most fellows got red-faced and shouted when they swore, Nevers had an understated way of drawling out his words that took everyone by surprise.

Windy said, "There's no question the boy's got a rare talent for swearing. The only fellow I ever knew who could match Nevers's style was an Irish pub master from Boston, and he had seventy years of practice."

Nevers's weak stomach also helped liven things up in the cookshack. One afternoon Ben and Nevers were trimming the wicks and washing the chimneys on the kerosene lamps. A chimney cracked in the dishwater, and Ben ran a sliver of glass into his finger.

"Dang nab it," Ben said as he pulled the sliver out. "Would you get me a clean handkerchief, Nevers?" Ben held his finger over the water and watched droplets of blood splash into the suds.

"What in blazes!" Pa said behind him.

Ben turned. Nevers had dropped to one knee, and he was white as a sheet. "I can't stand the sight of blood," he said.

"I might as well be working in an infirmary," Pa said, "with all the bleeding and fainting around here."

Another time, when Pa asked him to empty the spittoon, Nevers got so sick from looking at the gobby mess in the bottom of the can that he almost puked.

Packy, who opened the door just as Nevers began coughing and gagging, laughed and said, "That's not a very good way to be advertising your cooking, boy."

As much as the jacks liked Nevers, once they found out that he was queasy, one fellow or the other was always teasing him. Packy would say, "What's that you got there,

Jiggers?" and when Nevers turned, Jiggers would open his mouth wide to show his slimy tobacco chaw. Ben thought the teasing was funny until Swede got downright mean one evening and wedged a board against the outhouse door, leaving Nevers trapped inside for an hour. From then on Ben took Nevers's side.

On the second Friday in December Windy opened the cookshack door and hollered, "They're here, boys."

"The four-horse teamsters?" Ben asked.

"And the top loaders, too," Windy said.

Ben and Nevers ran outside to check, for that meant that the most important work of the winter—loading the massive logs onto sleds and hauling them to the river-bank—was about to begin.

That day the head teamster, Ed Day, and five other drivers checked in along with a half-dozen men in the loading and landing crews. The push also hired three road monkeys to help maintain the roads. Though two of them had experience, one of the boys was a gazebo named Ernie Gunderson. Gundy got lots of teasing. It started when the push asked him if he'd ever shoveled road apples. Gundy said, "Ain't it a little late in the season for apples?"

The push shook his head when he told Pa about it. "What's this world coming to when a boy don't know the difference between apples and horse manure?" The jacks thought it was so funny they called him Gundy Appleseed.

Ed Day was just the opposite. From the minute Ben saw him, he could tell that Ed was a teamster. He dressed in an ankle-length sheepskin coat rather than a wool mackinaw, and he wore four-buckle felt-topped overshoes, fur driving mitts, and a wool cap with earflaps. Ed was only average height, but he walked with a confident air that made him seem taller. Every other lumberjack in camp had a nickname, but the men simply called him Day.

The teamster's word was so trusted that the jacks went to him whenever they had a question. "Day says . . ." was all it took to end a squabble. Ben hoped he could work for Day sometime.

Day handled the horses with the same ease he had with the men. Ben had seen other teamsters whip their horses, but Day started his team by saying, "Walk, boys." If he wanted them to pull extra hard, he'd call, "Give her tar paper, you hay burners," and the horses would perk up their ears and lean forward.

As the head teamster, it was Day's job to supervise all the horses. When Ben asked him how he picked his teams, Day said, "You want to match 'em in size, gait, and personality. And though you wouldn't think it'd matter, I even factor in their color. A team that looks good pulls good."

Since Ben had always wanted to be a teamster, one day after supper he asked Pa, "How does a fellow get a teamster's job?"

"Same way as you learn to bake a pie. You practice."

"What your pa means," Day said as he got up from the table, "is that it don't matter whether you're pulling a plow or a freight wagon, just as long as you study horses. The way a horse takes a bit in his mouth, the way he tenses his flanks or lifts his hind feet can tell you a world about how he's feeling. I'd wager that you've learned a few things piloting the swingdingle."

"I learned to keep my seat while Old Dan rests on a hill."

"Then you're on your way to being a teamster." Day chuckled.

"For now, our Mister Would-be Teamster better be picking up these dishes," Pa said.

15

CHARLIE'S STORY, OR PUNTING ON THE CHERWELL

One Saturday morning Ben set down the breakfast tray and looked at Charlie.

"Are you waiting for something?" Charlie asked.

"Ain't you gonna finish that story about you waiting at the train station in Grand Rapids?"

"Don't you have to run back to the cookshack?"

"I'm not so rushed since Nevers hired on."

"Let me see." Charlie set his glasses on the table. "I believe I told you about arriving in Grand Rapids?"

"That's where you left off."

"On that particular day I was set on getting as far away from the civilized world as I could. That's why I'd bought a ticket to Pembina."

"And you said your problems were all due to a girl. But it wasn't that one." Ben pointed to a photo by the bookcase.

"You are an astute listener." Charlie grinned. "The girl I refer to was the daughter of a mathematics professor.

Back in Oxford I'd worked my way through school by singing in the choir and studying hard. You can't imagine how dull it is to spend your whole life translating old poems from Latin to English, but I'd done my A-level exams and won a scholarship to college. That's when the new professor arrived."

"I've read a few dull poems myself," Ben said. "Did that professor by any chance have a pretty daughter?"

"You guessed it. I fell for her hard, but her father was a mean bloke who despised commoners. He had hopes of his daughter marrying a titled man, but she and I saw each other in secret. One day I took her punting on the River Cherwell."

"What's punting?" Ben asked.

"A punt's a flat-bottomed boat that you pole along. If you pack a basket lunch, it makes for a romantic afternoon. Her father happened to walk across the bridge as we were returning to the boat works. He took a swing at me with his umbrella and slipped on the wet planking. I reached out to catch him, but we both tumbled into the river. That was the end of my Oxford career. A month later the girl announced her engagement to a nobleman from Kent. I packed up my books and headed for America."

"But how does that other gal figure in?" Ben asked.

"Remember how I told you that I was killing time at the station in Grand Rapids?"

Ben nodded.

"The train finally pulled in, and I climbed on board.

But I'd no sooner handed the conductor my ticket when I saw a pretty girl out of the corner of my eye. Something clicked inside me. I hollered, 'Hold the train,' and got right off."

"She must have been real pretty," Ben said.

"The truth is I only had one glance, yet I sensed she was something special. I introduced myself to her father and asked permission to speak with her. Her name was Lucinda Warren, and she'd just been hired as the teacher in Blackwater."

"'Why, isn't that a coincidence,' I said to her, 'I'm traveling to Blackwater, too.' At the time I had no clue where Blackwater was, but I would have bought a ticket to China if she'd been headed there."

A strange thought struck Ben. "Did anyone call her Lucy?"

"Some folks did. Is something wrong?"

Ben stood up and walked closer to the picture. "Did she always wear that necklace?"

"It was her favorite."

Ben thought back to the wedding picture on the wall back home. "And she was hired to teach in Blackwater?"

"What are you driving at?"

"My mother wore a necklace just like that," Ben said slowly. "And before she got married she was a teacher."

Charlie's eyes widened.

"I've never heard anyone call my mother anything but Lucy."

"Blimy O'Reilly!" Charlie's mouth dropped open and

his glasses nearly fell off the end of his nose. "Don't tell me your mum was Lucinda Warren?"

"And you were her beau!" Ben gaped at Charlie. It was even harder to imagine the filer going courting than it was to see him as a choirboy. Ben took a breath to steady himself. "Can you tell me what my mother was like? She died when I was real little."

"Died? Lucinda . . . gone?" Charlie stared at Ben. Then he turned away. When he finally looked up, he spoke slowly. "Of course, I'd heard that your pa was a widower. But I had no idea that—" He sighed. "And you sitting here and being her boy all along. It's too much to swallow at once." Charlie and Ben both fixed their eyes on the photograph for a long time.

"When did you start courting her?" Ben asked.

"I tried to win her hand from the first moment that I saw her. But your pa is the lucky man she married." Charlie stopped again. "The whole thing flabbergasts me."

"What sort of a lady was she?" Ben asked.

"Like I said before, she was real pretty. But she had more than good looks. You could call it grace or style."

Charlie waved toward his bookshelf. "A poem in one of my books comes closest to telling what she was like. It's called 'She Walks in Beauty.' Lucinda had a light in her eyes that could lift you off your feet."

"Whatever happened between the two of you?"

"Bennnn . . ." It was Pa yelling.

"Sorry"—Ben opened the door—"but I gotta go."

Charlie nodded.

Ben ran back to the cookshack. "Pa, you'll never guess what Charlie told me."

"Who cares what that cranky old dentist said? We ain't got time for guessing games around here, unless you plan on driving an empty swingdingle out to the cut and letting those loggers lunch on you."

Fine, Ben thought. This can stay between me and Charlie.

○ ○ ○

The next day Ben was so anxious to hear Charlie finish his story that he brought the man's lunch over a half hour early. Charlie began where he'd left off. "I had big hopes for me and Lucinda, but her father took to me more than she did. Her pa was so pleased to hear that I was going to Blackwater that he asked if I would look after his daughter. It was a big improvement over that blighter in Oxford knocking me into the River Cherwell."

"So you went to Blackwater?"

"That very day," Charlie said.

Just then Nevers tapped on the door. "Your pa asked me to get Old Dan, so you'd better hurry."

"I need to get cracking on these saws, anyway," Charlie said.

"Promise you'll finish telling the story?"

"Of course."

When Ben got back to the cookshack, Pa was talking to Nevers. "You do any teamstering in Carolina?"

"I've done some plowing," Nevers said, "but we favor smaller animals. Lots of farmers get by with a pair of mules."

"Mules are smart," Pa said, "but they could never move the tonnage of wood we need. Some camps use oxen, but that old saying *dumb as a ox* is true. Only advantage to an ox is it makes decent soup if it dies on the job."

Nevers was still laughing at Pa's joke when Ben walked in. "'Member that blind mule the Montgomerys owned?" Ben asked, trying to keep Pa in his good mood. "He could plow all day and all night, but Maggie went and sold him 'cause he kicked her cat in the head."

But Pa only said, "We'd better quit gabbing about livestock and get back to work, here."

THE DEACON'S BENCH

Nevers made his daily contributions to the hospital kitty without complaining until one Sunday. The trouble started when Jiggers reached in front of Packy and stabbed the last two sweat pads off Nevers's platter.

Packy looked mean at Jiggers and mumbled, *"Il faut savoir tirer parti du pire."*

Nevers marched back to the kitchen and spoke to Pa. "Packy's swearin' in French."

"How do you know he's swearin'?"

"Cussin' should cost a fellow a penny no matter what language it's in."

"French don't count," Pa said, "but I'm liable to start chargin' whiners a penny if you don't quit complainin'."

"I still say it ain't fair."

Because it was Sunday and Ben didn't have to get the swingdingle ready, he was hoping to quiz the dentist about his mother. But when Ben stepped inside the filer's shack, Charlie wouldn't even look up from his saw.

Ben looked at Charlie and then at the picture of

Lucinda Warren. Charlie finally said, "You waiting for something?"

"You promised you'd finish your story."

"Your father must know a lot more about your mum than me."

"Whenever I ask him, he always changes the subject."

"But your grandpa must have talked—" Charlie stopped. "I forgot that Lucy's father died, didn't he? I'll be. So you know absolutely nothing about your mother?"

Ben nodded.

"You can see for yourself she was lovely," Charlie said. "But the thing I admired most about Lucinda was her good humor and her grit. She was only seventeen the fall she started teaching in Blackwater. Some of the lads were twice her size, but that didn't make a whit of difference to her."

"And you followed her all the way there?" Ben asked.

"I was a bloody nutter for doing it." Charlie shook his head. "But there was something about her I couldn't resist. Looking back, I should've known better. The fact that her father took a liking to me was the kiss of death. You know how young folks are. If their parents want them to do a thing, they do the opposite." Charlie paused. "I tried everything I could to win her over. There were other fellows trying to court her, but I always got there first. I'd sweep out the schoolhouse. I'd take her to church. When there was a dance, I'd slick back my hair and dress up in a fancy evening coat that I'd brought from England. But Lucy never seemed to be impressed."

"Didn't you tell her how you felt?" Ben was trying

to imagine how different Charlie must have looked back then.

"I talked myself blue. And looking back, I can see that was another miscalculation."

"How do you mean?"

"She must have thought I was barmy. I told her I loved her every time I saw her. I bought her flowers and candy. I proposed marriage at least twice each week."

"Did she ever hint that she might say yes?" Ben asked.

"Whenever things started going well, her father wrote to her, asking how the handsome young Englishman was doing and if we'd set a date yet. His hints and me campaigning like I was in the final week of a parliamentary election got to be too much for her."

Ben tried to imagine what it would have been like to have an educated fellow like Charlie for his pa.

"Like a fool, I kept pressing," Charlie said. "One afternoon we got into an argument. I said, 'Either we get engaged right now or else.'"

"She said, 'Or else what?'"

"I was too proud to take it back. So I said, 'Or else I'm taking a job at a logging camp.'"

"'Have a good time,' she said."

"By the next day I realized I'd been daft, but I headed to a camp in Silverdale anyway. That winter I figured I'd teach her a lesson by never writing a single letter."

"Is that when you learned to be a filer?" Ben asked.

"Filer?" Charlie laughed. "I was the most useless logger you've ever seen. The push tried me at every job in camp. He finally settled on road monkey. All I'd known at Oxford was singing and studying."

"Did you ever go back to see her?"

"After the spring breakup I got spiffed up and planned on surprising her. But on my way to a dance a fellow told me that Lucy was engaged to another man—that must have been your pa." Charlie looked down at his bench and tapped his file. "I balled up my swallowtail coat and threw it into the river."

"Is that when you decided not to take any more baths?"

Charlie smiled sadly. "It wasn't as if I decided to give up bathing on a certain day. First I stopped shaving. Then I stopped buying new clothes. Pretty soon I'd worked a whole winter without setting foot in the boiling-up shack. Instead of heading to town that spring, I signed on as a summer watchman. For one stretch I stayed in the woods eleven straight years."

"Weren't you lonesome?"

"Nary once. It's peaceful out here in the summer. There's fishing and berry picking. Best of all, a fellow's got time to read and think. Another writer named Henry David Thoreau—he was one of your mum's favorites—summarized it best when he said, 'I never found the companion that was so companionable as solitude.'

"That fall I hired on as a lumberjack again, and an old Scotsman taught me the filer's trade. Since those fellows tend to be secretive, I was flattered that he showed me his technique. He must have known he didn't have much time left. He passed on the next summer."

"What's the big secret about saw filing?"

"There's more to sharpening a misery whip than putting an edge on the steel," Charlie said. "Before I start, I want to know the temperature, humidity, and the kind of wood the saw will be used on."

"Like if you're cutting oak or pine?"

"I try to be even more exact. I set the teeth a little differently depending on whether the jacks will be in red or white pine.

"Speaking of filing, I'd better get back to my sharpening, or the boys will be knocking my door down tomorrow morning."

Later that afternoon Ben and Nevers walked down to the bunkhouse. Since Ben couldn't stand keeping Charlie's courting a secret anymore, he told Nevers.

"Go on," Nevers said.

"I'm serious."

Nevers turned to Ben, talking fast for a change. "You mean to tell me that ole coot coulda been your daddy?"

"Charlie said he used to dress up real fancy and go to country dances," Ben said.

"I wouldn't let that man into a barn dance if the cows were still inside," Nevers said. "You fixin' to tell your pa?"

"He don't care."

"Your pa cares more than you think." Ben was about

to ask Nevers what he meant when Nevers asked, "Is this a dry camp?"

"The push don't allow no liquor."

"Good," Nevers said. "At my last camp whenever the boys got liquored up a fight would start."

"Jacks and drinking don't mix," Ben agreed. "We had a fellow named Bill Malone rooming at Mrs. Wilson's. No one knew he was a drinker until Mrs. Wilson got called to the doctor's office one evening. Bill was so kegged up he'd mistook a mannequin for a pretty girl and jumped through the dress shop window. Had twenty stitches across his cheek and arm." Ben paused. "That reminds me that I haven't got Mrs. Wilson her Christmas present yet."

"Presents is scarcer than hens' teeth out here," Nevers said. "What'd you get her last year?"

"A little mirror," Ben said. "But the pencil pusher's got nothing but clothes and jackknives in his store."

"You could make her something," Nevers said.

"How would I do that?"

"There was a carpenter—the only decent fellow at the orphanage—who showed me some woodworking projects."

"Do you think we could find some wood?"

"This here's a lumber camp, ain't it?" Nevers said.

As the boys neared the bunkhouse, Nevers asked, "Do any of the jacks dose themselves?"

"A few buy patent medicines from the pencil pusher," Ben said. "They complain of everything from rheumatism to heart palpitations, but they'll buy any ole bottle that has alcohol in it. Arno's favorite brand is Dr. Bingham's Liver Tonic. He claims it eases a shoulder ache, but I've noticed his pain magically shifts from here to here." Ben jabbed Nevers in the right shoulder and then the left.

"Cut that out," Nevers said, poking him back.

When Ben opened the door, Windy called, "Hey, Benny Boy. Looks like you brought your new helper."

Packy's eyes lit up when he saw Nevers. "Hi there, second cookee. *Tout ce qui brille n'est pas or.*"

"Cut that out," Nevers said. "Cussing at me in the cookshack is bad enough."

"*En Avril ne te découvre pas d'un fil,*" Packy shot back.

Nevers turned to Windy. "Tell him to stop."

"Packy can talk any language he wants in this bunkhouse."

"Just ignore him," Ben said. "And be careful where you sit. Every deacon's bench is shared by the two fellows who have the nearest bunks. That one looks open." He pointed beside Windy.

"You look a little glum today," Windy said to Ben.

"Pa's been crabby lately."

"Crabby!" Jiggers laughed from the card table. "Jack Ward is the most gentlemanly cook I've ever met."

"Nevers said the same thing."

"He's right," Jiggers said. "I knew a cook who tossed a meat cleaver at a jack. He missed his target and clipped the earlobe off an innocent fellow who was sipping his swamp water."

"Pa seems plenty grouchy to me," Ben said.

"Jack is a talented flapjack flipper, too," Windy said. "Try working off the Gut and Liver Line Railroad sometime. The cook is a short fellow named Mickey Mannheim who serves nothing but wieners and liver."

Ben and Nevers made faces.

"But the worst cooks are the drunks," Packy said, dealing the next hand of cards. "You never can tell what they're gonna throw into the kettle. One time at Rory Calhoun's camp I found a sock in the teapot. When I brought it to Rory's attention, he said, 'Thanks, Frenchy, I wondered where that sock went.' "

"Rory was a fine cook when he was straight," Jiggers agreed, "but he'd only stay sober until he had time to batch up some home brew out of raisins and prunes and pie crust."

"You believe your pa ain't so bad now?" Nevers poked Ben in the arm.

"He's still crabby, if you ask me," Ben said.

"Which fellow is your wood butcher?" Nevers asked.

Ben pointed him out at the card table.

Nevers walked up to him and asked, "Would you have a board to spare for a Christmas project?"

"Fine by me. Arno burns up the waste oak in his forge anyway. After I finish this game, I'll let you borrow some tools."

"We're set." Nevers grinned at Ben. "I've made some fine projects out of hickory, and oak should polish up about the same. Give us a couple Sundays, and Santa'll be coming to the Blackwater Logging Camp."

THE SKY HOOK

Over the next few days Ben found out more about his mother from Charlie. He learned that her favorite color was green (so was Ben's), and that she loved rainstorms (Ben didn't) and lemon meringue pie (a match again). One of her favorite books was *Walden*. Charlie explained that it was by Thoreau, the fellow he'd mentioned once before, who had loved nature so much that he'd built a little cabin in the woods and lived there all by himself. She also liked a story called *Le Morte d'Arthur*, which didn't sound good until Charlie told him it was about King Arthur and his knights.

The problem was every time the dentist started a good story, Ben got called back to the cookshack. Even with Nevers's help, there were so many new jacks arriving in camp that the kitchen crew scrambled to keep up.

Luckily, Ben was getting faster at his potato peeling, thanks to the tater races he and Nevers were having. Nevers usually won their one-potato duels, but when it came to endurance peeling—doing a whole panful at a time—Ben came out on top as often as Nevers did.

Despite Nevers's quickness in the kitchen, he often got in trouble for not keeping track of supplies. Pa had a paper stuck on the wall, and the cookees were supposed to mark down items that were low. But because Nevers couldn't write, he had to ask Ben to do his recording.

Whenever there was a mistake, Pa knew where to turn. "How come this lard can is near empty," he said once, looking straight at Nevers, "and I don't see no note on our order list?"

"I'll take care of it, Pa," Ben said.

If they weren't in too big of a hurry, Ben showed Nevers how to write simple words like *salt* and *pork*. But when it came to *rutabagas* or *molasses,* Ben had enough trouble spelling those himself.

"Thanks, Ben," Nevers said after he'd printed out *oleo* for the first time. "You're a good teacher."

"Don't call me that," Ben said, shivering at the thought of being compared to the helmet-haired, ruler-wielding Miss Stanish.

❍ ❍ ❍

Of all the new arrivals, the jack who impressed Ben the most was Percy Cantwell. Cantwell was a lanky top loader known as Slim, though some of the fellows called him Sky Hook. Slim had cool gray eyes, and he didn't joke around like the other fellows. When Ben asked Windy why Slim never strung more than a half dozen words together, Windy said, "Slim is one jack who lets his loading do his talking. It takes a special touch to top off a sled that's decked out with twenty thousand feet of wood."

No matter how cold it got, Slim wore a short jacket. His staged pants had been cut off above the ankles so the cuffs couldn't trip him up, and his leather boots were fitted with low lumbermen's overshoes for good traction. Slim preferred a Stetson hat over the usual wool cap.

The first time Ben saw Slim at work, he understood what Windy meant about Slim's loading doing his talking. The crews hadn't moved a stick of timber to the landing yet, and Ben knew that if the logs couldn't be floated downstream in the spring, the company wouldn't get paid. But once Ben saw Slim working on a load, he knew it would be a cinch for them to make their contract.

Ben had just pulled up to the cut, but nobody noticed him. Since the jacks normally ran the minute they saw the lunch sled, Ben thought something was wrong. Then he saw that everyone was watching Slim.

When Ben climbed down, Ed Day pointed at the loading crew. "The groundhogs are sending a blue butt up to the Sky Hook."

Ben knew that the groundhogs or sending-up men were the fellows who guided the logs up the skid poles that leaned against the sled. He asked Day, "What's a blue butt?"

"Log with a big bell," Day said. "Taper makes 'em tough to control. Some call 'em big blues. They can be two-ton killers if you don't know your stuff."

Slim was straddling the top of a two-story-tall load. Logging sleds were dangerous because the logs were held in place only with corner binds and wrapper chains. The whole load could be dumped by two men hammering loose the fid hooks, U-shaped pieces of iron that held the chains.

Slim was about to top off the load with a monster log. The groundhogs had wrapped a rope around the blue butt, and the cross-haul teamster was ready to pull from the other side.

At a signal from Slim, the teamster started his horses. As the log rolled up the skids, the groundhogs guided each end, while Slim stood on top with his cant hook in his hand and a pipe jutting out of his mouth. "He's always got that stub pipe between his teeth," Day said. "You can tell how hard he's concentrating by the angle of the pipe stem."

Ben figured this must be a tricky load, for as the log shot up the skids, Slim's jaw tightened, and his pipe stood straight up. "Saginaw," Slim hollered from between his clenched teeth.

"What's that mean?" Ben asked.

"They need to slow the small end of the log. But if Slim says St. Croix, it's time to speed her up."

The icy bark crackled as the log climbed the skid poles. It was traveling so fast that it looked like it would shoot over the top and crush Slim.

Just when Ben was ready to holler "Jump!" Slim cut the log free. Dancing aside, he buried his cant hook in the butt end and gave the log a quarter of a turn. The momentum was perfect. The blue butt settled onto the top of the load with a resounding thunk. Ben heard that same sound whenever he watched cabin builders roll a perfectly scribed log into place. As flecks of bark and ice fell to the ground, the jacks nodded their approval.

"I don't think we'll need to chain this one down 'tall," Slim said, walking the length of the massive log to test its balance. Slim's pipe was back to horizontal, and he wore a hint of a smile.

Slim took his pipe out of his mouth and pointed to Ben. "Now that cookee's here, we'd better take ourselves a lunch break."

The Norwegian Helper and
How One Monkey Got Sent Down the Road

When Ben arrived at the cut the next day, the jacks were lined up before he could climb down from his seat. As Ben opened the food box, Packy whispered, "Want to see something funny?"

"I suppose." Was Packy going to play a trick on him?

"I'll wait till you have the boys ladled up."

Instead of sitting on the log with the rest of the men, Packy sneaked up behind Jiggers.

When Jiggers lifted a spoonful of beans to his mouth, Packy let out a wolf howl.

Jiggers jumped straight up. His spoon flew out of his hand, and his plate flipped over. The jacks laughed as beans, pie, and bread scattered in all directions.

The only man who didn't laugh was Swede. He paused only long enough to scrape a few stray beans off his pants leg and shovel them into his mouth.

"Dang you, reprobate," Jiggers yelled at Packy. Then he turned to Ben. "You got any extra grub in that pot?"

"I've never seen anybody jump so high," Ben said as

he scooped some cold beans from the bottom of the kettle. He was surprised that Jiggers wasn't angrier.

"I can't help myself," Jiggers said. "When I get startled, it's like a trigger goes off inside me."

"He's some jumper, eh?" Packy laughed.

While Ben was loading the dishes, he got a chance to see the sawyers work up close for the first time. The swampers had already cleared the brush around a big pine, and the notcher had chopped off the bark at the cut line. Without saying a word, the sawyers set their saw in place. After a few short strokes to start the blade, they pulled in a steady rhythm that made the taut steel sing. The teeth spilled long curls of white wood out of the kerf, and the resin smell of pine prickled Ben's nose.

Halfway through the cut the sawyers stopped and hammered two wedges into the kerf to keep the blade from binding. Packy said, "You'd better clear the road, cookee."

"Let me show him my Norwegian helper first." Swede waved to Ben from the opposite side of the road. "Come over and meet my little buddy."

Ben looked at the pine Swede was ready to fell. There was no one else in sight. "He's right here," Swede said. Bending down, he plucked a rubber cord that was looped around an iron stake pounded into the ground. "How do you like my helper?" He chuckled.

Swede grabbed the handle of his saw. Each time he pulled the blade toward him, the cord drew it back. He was sawing faster than the two-man crew. "Those foremen never have found a man who could keep up with me."

"But don't it get lonely?" Ben asked.

"Where could I find better company than me?" Swede said. "Besides, I never have to argue with anyone when it's just me"—he plucked the cord—"and my buddy."

Ben shook his head as he walked to the swingdingle. He'd never met anyone more in love with himself than Swede.

As Ben was picking up the reins, Ed Day hollered, "Pull, boys, pull." Ben looked up just in time to see a road monkey jump clear of Day's sled. The monkeys were supposed to shovel the manure off the road and spread hay on the hills to slow the sled runners, but this boy had forgotten to shake the frost out of the hay.

Day's sled raced down the icy ruts like a runaway train. The logs swayed as Day hollered, "Ho, Buddy," to his lagging leader. The horses couldn't run any faster, but the sled was still picking up speed. It would tear Day's heart to see his prize animals sluiced. Just when Ben thought the team was going to fall under the runners, the sled jumped the ruts and headed for the woods. It missed a birch tree but snapped off a small balsam. A shower of needles flew into the air, and Day's cap got knocked into the snow, but his horses kept their feet as the sled jerked to a stop.

Day ran forward to check his team. Only then did he turn and yell, "You, monkey, you—" But he stopped when he saw that the boy was already hightailing it back to camp. "That monkey might not know much about haying," Day said, grinning, "but he knows when it's time to collect his pay."

When Ben told Nevers about the accident on the hill, Nevers's eyes got big. "I seen a horse go down once under a runaway wagon," he said, "and it ain't pretty."

"Did the horse get killed?"

"Tore him up something awful. It was my daddy's best plow horse, Jefferson Davis. He'd loaned him to a neighbor who got liquored up and drove his lumber wagon down a muddy hill over the top of him. Poor Jeff was such a mess you couldn't tell the red clay from the blood. We only had a two-horse farm, so that cut our stock in half."

"Did your neighbor pay for the horse?" Ben asked.

"You cain't get blood from a turnip. Looking back, I can see that was the beginning of the end of my daddy's farming days. And in the long run, it was the end of his marriage days, too."

JIGGERS JUMPS AGAIN

O nce Packy knew that he could get under Nevers's skin by speaking French, he teased him every chance he got. Sometimes he'd walk into the cookshack and say, "Hello there, Nevers." Then, after Nevers had relaxed, he'd spew, *"En Avril ne te découvre pas d'un fil,"* at him. Other times Packy wouldn't say a word the whole meal, but when Nevers was serving the dessert, he'd whisper, *"Vivre et laisser vivre."*

"Make him stop, Mr. Ward," Nevers said, but Pa and the rest of the jacks only laughed.

"Don't let Packy rile you up like that," Ben said. "The more excited you get, the more he's gonna do it."

"But—" Nevers started.

"Your partner's right," Slim cut in. "It don't do no good to throw kerosene on a fire."

By Sunday Ben was looking forward to having extra time with Charlie. Ben had tried asking Pa questions

106

about his mother, but he'd only grumbled, "She was a fine lady. What else can I say?"

As Ben made up a lunch tray for Charlie, Nevers asked, "Suppose he'll tell you more about your ma?"

"He's contrary at times, but I hope so."

"Come and get me when you're done, and we'll get started on our woodworking."

Ben knocked on the dentist's door, and Charlie greeted him with the closest he'd ever come to a smile. "How's Squire Benjamin?"

"Isn't *squire* some sort of fancy title?"

"*Squire* used to refer to a country gentleman, but these days we use it to mean any young working man."

"That's me, then. I'm young and I work."

After talking about the weather and camp life, Ben finally said, "So what else can you tell me about my mother?"

"Did I tell you how feisty Lucinda was?" Charlie looked over the top of his glasses. "She loved to talk ideas. She could have taken on an Oxford debate team single-handed, especially when she was talking about *Walden*."

"The book about that fellow who lived alone in the woods?"

Charlie nodded. "She could quote *Walden* backwards and forwards. I hadn't studied Thoreau in England, so he was new to me. Thoreau believed in independent thinking and in folks following their dreams.

"Lucy and I had a long discussion over the end of the book. After spending two years in his shack, Thoreau went back to town. I told her that if he was true to his beliefs, he should have stayed at Walden, but she insisted that he'd learned all he could and needed to move on."

"So he decided to give people a try again."

"You could say so," Charlie said, looking toward his saws. "Sunday might be a holiday for you, but it's the only day these misery whips sit idle. I'd better get cracking."

Ben and Nevers spent the rest of the afternoon working on Christmas presents for Pa and Mrs. Wilson. After running through a list of projects that they could make out of scrap wood using only hand tools—"I figure that eliminates a rolltop desk or a credenza," Ben said—they decided on a bird feeder for Mrs. Wilson and a cutting board for Pa.

Ben came up with the idea of making the feeder look like a rough model of Mrs. Wilson's boardinghouse, and Nevers suggested attaching small leather hinge strips on the roof so that it would be easy to add bird seed.

Nevers traced out a scalloped pattern on Pa's cutting board, which made it a lot fancier than a plain hunk of wood. Then they took turns cutting out the rough shape with a keyhole saw and rasping the edges smooth. For a final touch, Ben and Nevers carved their initials in the handle along with the date: 1898.

After supper the boys visited the bunkhouse. Packy greeted them by saying, "Howdy, fellows." Then, after pausing just long enough to get Nevers off his guard, he added, *"Mieux vaut tard que jamais."*

Nevers was about to spout something back at Packy,

but Ben touched his arm and said, "Don't let him get your dander up."

Slim winked at Ben from the card table.

The rest of the jacks were sitting quietly. The room was lit by the hazy glow of two hanging kerosene lanterns. Ben whispered to Nevers, "Do you want to see something funny?"

"Okay," Nevers said.

"You keep Jiggers's attention for a minute."

Ben sneaked up behind Jiggers, who was sitting in a chair with his feet facing the stove.

"What you working on?" Nevers asked.

"I'm just whittling," Jiggers said.

"Boo!" Ben yelled. Jiggers jumped straight up. Ben was ready to laugh until he saw the knife. Before Ben could duck, the blade flew out of Jiggers's hand and buried itself in the log support post.

Jiggers stared at the bone-handled hunting knife that had stuck in the wood right between Ben's and Nevers's cheeks. Instead of yelling, Jiggers asked, "You all right?"

Ben and Nevers both nodded.

"You *imbécile*," Packy said, cuffing Ben's arm. "He coulda killed any one of us."

"I wasn't thinking," Ben said when he finally found his voice.

When Packy saw that Ben and Nevers were both pale and shaking, he put his arms around their shoulders. "At least you dopes are okay. If Jiggers had been holding an ax in his hand, somebody woulda got guillotined for sure."

CHRISTMAS AND THE GOOD SISTERS, OR
THE NUN AND THE BLUE BUTTS

The tote teamster arrived two days before Christmas. Ben was excited to see that Pa's special order had come along with the mail and the regular supplies.

"The turkeys are here!" Ben called back to the kitchen. Pa needed a dozen turkeys for Christmas dinner, and he'd been worried all week that they might not arrive in time.

When the teamster headed back to town, Ben sent along the bird feeder that he and Nevers had made. He tied it inside a flour sack and put a tag on it that said MERRY CHRISTMAS, MRS. WILSON. FROM: BEN AND NEVERS.

On Christmas Eve Charlie gave Ben one of his books as a present. That was a much better gift than the new white shirt from Pa! It was a copy of *Le Morte d'Arthur,* the King Arthur story his mother had liked. Charlie read him a short part about Arthur claiming his right to the throne. Charlie's accent made the legend seem so real that Ben could imagine himself grabbing the hilt of the magical sword Excalibur and pulling it from an anvil anchored in rock.

Ben was running back from the dentist's shack with

Charlie's dishes in one hand and his book in the other when a little sleigh drove up to the cookshack. Ben was so anxious to tell Nevers about his King Arthur book that it took him a minute to realize that the cutter was carrying two ladies.

Should he warn the push? Along with his no gambling and no liquor rules, the push had a strict policy against women visiting the camp. Since the ladies were wearing mackinaws, Ben didn't see their robes until they climbed out. "You're nuns!" Ben blurted out.

The taller one, who was at least six feet, turned to Ben. "Were you expecting carnival freaks? Do us a favor, sonny, and take our horse down to the barn." She banged on the door and hollered, "What's for dinner, you old hash slinger?"

Pa opened the door and grinned. "If it ain't Sister Aggie!" he said. "It's been a long time." They gave each other a hug. "I figured you'd come sooner now that you've opened up that new hospital in Grand Rapids."

"It's a shorter haul," the sister said, "but this ragtag outfit ain't the only camp in the north woods."

"I can't believe all the years you traveled from Duluth to visit us jacks."

"Who else would sell hospital tickets to you clumsy boys who are doing your best to chop your feet off?" The sister smiled. Ben was shocked to hear a nun talk so casually, and he was even more shocked at how forward Pa was. "By the way," the sister said, "I'd like you to meet my new helper, Sister Gwen."

The younger nun said, "Nice to meet you, sir."

"And these are my cookees," Pa said. "My son, Ben, and young Nevers here. Meet Sister Agnes, boys."

"Call me Aggie, please. By looking at Ben, I can tell that the apple don't fall far from the tree." She dug Pa in the ribs and winked.

"Can I interest you ladies in a little dinner?"

"Why, thank you, Mr. Ward," Sister Gwen replied.

"It better be more than a little dinner, Jack Ward," Sister Aggie said. "Driving that old nag stirs up my appetite."

"I'll do my best to put something together." Pa smiled.

"Any meal is bound to be an improvement over our last camp," Sister Aggie said, scrunching up her face. "That half-soused cook served up venison ribs that were so tallowy we couldn't hardly part our lips to sing those jacks a hymn."

The younger sister giggled.

"You came at the right time if you're in the mood for some serious eating, Sister," Pa said. "We're having roast turkey tomorrow, and we're baking up a pie for every single man."

"And for every woman, I hope!" Then Sister Aggie nodded toward Ben. "Does that cookee of yours suffer from an addlepated brain?"

"What's wrong with him?"

"I gave him directions to take care of my horse, but he's still standing there with his mouth hanging open."

"Sorry, Pa," Ben said. "I'll bring her cutter to the barn."

When Ben got back inside, Pa looked at Nevers and said, "I believe you have something for the sisters."

"I do?"

"Ain't you been the main contributor to the hospital kitty?"

"I guess so." Nevers blushed.

"Jack hired himself a cussing cookee, eh?" Sister Aggie said.

"I'm sorry, ma'am. But the words just pop out," Nevers said as he lugged the can over and set it on the table.

"Well, son, you need to understand that God's name is not to be taken in—" Sister Aggie stopped when she tried to lift the can. She looked inside. "Lord sakes alive! Have you got the whole U.S. mint canned up here?" She patted Nevers on the shoulder. "I'd say that you've done your full penance already. Just watch that mouth in the future."

"Yes, ma'am."

Later, as Ben and Nevers were helping Pa get a meal together for the sisters, Nevers looked nervous.

"What's wrong?" Ben asked.

"I'm afraid the jacks'll be impolite to those nuns."

"You've got nothing to worry about," Pa said.

"We never had women stop by my other camps."

"Around here even the rowdiest jacks show proper manners where women are concerned," Pa said. "One day a jack in Blackwater named Big Willy went snaky on bad moonshine and started digging a hole in the middle of Main Street. Some fellows tried to wrestle his shovel away, but he was too big and strong. Willy kept cussing and mumbling,

'Ain't nobody gonna jump my claim. This here's my gold.' But when Mrs. Wilson came by, Willy took off his cap and said, 'Good afternoon, ma'am.' He waited until she passed before he went back to his digging."

Sure enough, the jacks were respectful through the whole meal. Pa suspended his no talking rule after supper, and the sisters led everyone in singing Christmas carols. Then Slim started a collection by dropping two bits into a lard bucket and saying, "Dig deep, boys."

Every jack also bought a hospital ticket from Sister Aggie. If they didn't have cash, the pencil pusher marked it down against their account. But when it came time for Nevers to pay, Sister Aggie put her arm around him and said, "This boy and I have already settled up."

During the singing Ben noticed that the only fellow who wasn't having any fun was Ernie Gunderson. Poor Gundy sat in the back corner all by himself. He had one of his sweetheart's letters out, and he just kept staring at it.

To the Races: Graybacks and Jacks

fter the collecting was done and the jacks had retired to the bunkhouse, Ben and Nevers got out Pa's present. "We didn't have a chance to wrap it," Ben said, "but we made it special for your kitchen."

"So when did you become a woodworker?" Pa asked.

"Nevers and I made it together," Ben said.

"This is real fine work, boys." Pa ran his hand along the edge. "And you even carved your initials."

"You can test it out tomorrow," Nevers said.

"I should say not," Pa said. "I'm hanging this cutting board right up on the wall where everybody can see it."

Picking up after supper went faster than usual because the sisters and Pa all helped. After they finished, Pa said, "Me and my cookees will sleep in the bunkhouse tonight so you ladies can have some privacy."

"That ain't necessary, Jack," Sister Aggie said.

"It's lots cleaner in here, and we don't mind, do we, boys?"

Ben and Nevers both said, "No, ma'am."

"If you insist," Sister Aggie said as Pa gathered up some blankets and handed them to the boys.

Ben and Nevers walked down ahead of Pa. "I've been wanting to try the bunkhouse all year long," Ben said.

"How come?" Nevers asked.

"For once I'd like to track some dirt in without getting yelled at."

Nevers frowned, but he didn't say anything more.

When the boys walked into the bunkhouse, Ben was surprised to see everyone clustered in front of Arno's bunk. The room smelled of wet socks, horse sweat, and liniment.

"Let's see what they're doin'," Ben said.

The jacks were staring at something in Jiggers's lap. Ben and Nevers looked over the shoulders of the men. Jiggers had a sheet of brown paper on his knee, and a circle was drawn in the middle.

"Ready?" Jiggers said, digging at his scalp.

Arno, who was picking in his own hair, said, "Yep."

Then he and Arno held their hands over the paper as Windy counted, "One, two, three, go!"

Jiggers and Arno each dropped a little white bug into the center of the circle, and the fellows all cheered. They were having a louse race!

Arno's louse just lay sideways on the paper, but Jiggers's hopped toward the outside of the circle. The minute Jiggers's bug crossed the line, Jiggers stood up and yelled, "I win!"

"No fair," Arno said, grabbing the paper and staring at the bug he'd dropped from his head. "Mine is dead."

"I can't help it if you're so clumsy you crushed it. That makes two out of three races I won fair and square."

While half of the fellows dug in their pockets to pay up their bets, Poultice Pete said to Arno, "I ain't never putting money on you again."

"Have you ever seen anything so disgusting?" Ben said to Nevers, but his friend was gone. "Where's Nevers?" Ben asked Windy.

Windy nodded toward the door. "I think that grayback racing upset his stomach."

Ben turned. Nevers, his face white as an eggshell, was kneeling on the stoop, taking a big gulp of fresh air.

"Shut the door, you dummy," Swede said. "If we ever have a puking contest around here, my money's gonna be on Nevers." The jacks had a good laugh.

Ben went out to help Nevers. "Just stand a minute," Ben said. "This cold air will clear your head."

"Freeze it, more likely," Nevers said.

When they stepped back inside, Swede said, "Hey, Nevers. Arno can save a few crushed lice if you'd like to sprinkle some on your oatmeal in the morning."

"Don't pay him no mind," Slim said.

Windy showed Ben and Nevers to their bunks at the far end of the room. "Before you boys sit down, let me run through the bunkhouse rules with you."

"I heard those rules a hundred times," Ben said.

"You hush and listen unless you want to sleep in a snowbank. The main and most important thing to remember is there ain't no spitting on the stove." He acted like he was reciting the Ten Commandments. "You use this here box"—Windy spit into the sandbox under the stove as an example—"or this here spittoon." Windy bent to spit into the pail, but he hesitated.

"What's the trouble, Santa Claus?" Packy laughed. "Did all that talking dry you out?"

By the time Windy was done, Pa had arrived. "Looks like we won't be sweating tonight," Pa said.

"What do you mean?" Ben looked at the red-hot stove.

"Watch this." Pa leaned into the corner and blew.

When Pa's breath turned to frost, Nevers's eyes widened. "You suppose we shoulda brung more blankets?"

As the jacks got ready for bed, each fellow followed his own routine. Packy unwound his sash and folded it neatly and set it on the deacon's bench below his bunk. Poultice Pete took off his long underwear, turned it inside out, and then put it back on again. "Poultice does that every night," Swede said. "It's his way of keeping clean. But I favor this." Swede lifted up his flour-sack pillow and showed Ben a half stick of dynamite.

"You sleep with dynamite under your head!" Ben said.

"The powder smell gives me a little headache, but it drives all the bugs away."

"I keep telling that fool a jolt of lightning's gonna hit this shack and blow us all to kingdom come," Jiggers said, "but he don't never listen."

When Windy called, "Lights out," and turned off the kerosene lamps, Ben heard the wind whistling between the logs. He rolled out his blanket on the loose hay, and the smell of tar paper and hot steel burned his nostrils. Ben wondered how many millions of lice were crawling around the bunkhouse. His neck felt itchy. To make matters worse, the stink of onions and turpentine was drifting up from Poultice Pete's bunk.

Ben was about to ask Nevers how he was doing when he heard a squeak. Then something tickled his lips. Thinking it was a bug, Ben tried to swat it, but before he could get his hand out from under the blankets, a little tail brushed across his cheek. "Pa!" Ben smacked at the place where he'd heard the critter dive into the hay. "A mouse ran over my face!"

"Shut your trap," Arno said from two bunks over, "or that little squeaker might jump into your mouth."

"Yuck." Nevers shivered in the bunk beside Ben.

Now it was Ben's turn to feel like throwing up.

"He won't hurt you none." Pa laughed. "You just rousted him out when you settled into the hay."

For the first time all winter, Ben appreciated how clean Pa kept the cookshack.

"Pa?" Ben asked.

"What now?"

"Could we stop in the boiling-up shack before we go back to our own beds?"

"I second the motion," Nevers called.

"Fine by me," Pa said. Ben felt him smiling in the dark.

"Hush up down there," Windy growled.

Soon the wind was overshadowed by the raspy

snoring, burps, and grosser noises of the lumberjacks. It sounded like the roof was ready to fly off.

Nevers whispered, "These fellows sure do rattle the tar paper, don't they?"

"Would you boys shut yer yaps?" Ed Day spoke from somewhere between Ben and Windy. "It'll be time to harness up soon."

From then on no one made a peep. The snoring got louder as the last of the men dozed off, but Ben lay awake, listening for another squeak or rustle. If a mouse touched his face again, he was going to rake the straw out of his bunk and sleep on bare wood.

❍ ❍ ❍

"Daylight in the swamp." Ben felt someone tap his shoulder.

Ben opened his eyes. He could barely make out Windy's beard in the dim light. It was four A.M. and time to start breakfast. Pa and Nevers were already slipping on their pants.

Ben dressed and laced up his boots. He felt a little dizzy from lack of sleep. Along with the snoring, the heavier jacks had made the bunk frames creak every time they rolled over. And once the man next to Ben had rapped the snorting pole between the bunks so hard that Ben sat straight up and bumped his head.

Ben pulled up his sleeve and scratched his forearm. Pa whispered, "Did the lice lunch on you last night?"

Ben nodded. The welts on his arm burned like blisters.

"Try not to scratch too much," Pa said. "We'll get over to the boiling-up shack as soon as we can."

As the three of them tiptoed out of the bunkhouse and into the bright moonlight, the rest of the jacks continued to snore. Outside, the wind had died, but the air was biting cold. Ben started to button up his shirt, but Pa said, "Don't bother. We'll shake our things out before we go inside."

Pa stood on the top step of the bunkhouse and stripped off his pants and underwear. Steam rose from his skin. "Stand on the toes of your boots so you don't freeze yourselves," he said as he shook out his clothes. He had just pulled his pants back on when the door swung open behind them. Ben and Nevers were whipping their woolies in the frigid air.

Lantern light streamed over the bare bottoms of the boys. "Morning, gentlemen," Sister Aggie said.

"Good mornin', Sister." Pa chuckled. "You're up early."

Ben and Nevers scrambled to dress while Pa stepped inside, still laughing.

"You realize a nun has just seen us naked?" Nevers groaned.

"How are we ever gonna face her?" Ben said.

The boys finally got tired of shivering in the dark and opened the door. They tried to slip in unnoticed, but Sister Aggie, who was working next to Pa, hollered, "Come on in, boys. And don't you be embarrassed. Being that I'm a nurse, I've seen hundreds of scrawny hinders in my day."

Ben didn't know if that made him feel better or worse.

But Nevers was suddenly excited. "Is that biscuits I smell?"

"And gravy," Sister Aggie said. "I figured I'd treat these Scandahoovians to a little Southern-style cooking for a change." She slapped Pa's hand away from her pan. "By the way you talk, boy, I'd wager you're from Georgia."

"South Carolina," Nevers said.

"My mother was a Tidewater gal," Sister said. "How'd you ever find your way to these parts?"

Nevers looked at Ben. Sister could tell that Nevers was wondering if it was safe to share his story with her. She chuckled, "I'm not about to turn you in, boy. If I tattled to the law about everything I knew, there wouldn't be a lumberjack left in these woods."

"Thank you, ma'am," Nevers said. "I'd sure hate to get sent back to that ole orphanage."

"Who wants the first biscuit?" Sister Aggie held one out.

"Go ahead, Nevers." Ben nudged him forward.

Nevers took a bite and smiled. "Merry Christmas!"

BOILING UP

As soon as the sisters left, Pa and the boys headed for the boiling-up shack. Now that the weather had turned cold, Poultice Pete was about the only jack who took a bath. But no matter how bitter it got, Ben and Nevers still had to go to the boiling-up shack once a week and launder the aprons and towels, and Pa insisted that he and his cookees bathe.

Ben had gone down earlier in the day and started a fire in the stove, because it took a couple of hours to heat enough water to fill the washtub.

Pa slipped off his clothes and took the first turn in the tub. "If we had a few Finlanders around here, there'd be more fellows who cared about keeping themselves clean," he said. Ben had heard that camps with Finnish men often built a separate sauna for bathing.

"We'd also have to eat fish soup," Nevers said.

"That's true." Pa chuckled. He looked at Nevers, who was sitting on the bench next to Ben. "Do you miss Carolina now that we're getting a touch of winter?"

Nevers nodded. "I get most lonesome at Christmas."

"I can understand that. Ben and I lost Lucy about this time of the year. It was the week after New Year's."

To Ben's surprise, Pa kept talking as he sudsed up his arms. "She caught a sudden fever. Ben was only two at the time. Lucy had doted on Ben since the day he was born. When we first got married, I was afraid that she wouldn't be happy giving up her teaching job. She wanted to tell the school board that it wasn't right to fire a gal the minute she took a husband, but she decided there was no use fighting. I still remember her standing with her hands on her hips and her dark eyes flashing. 'All that school board does is talk policy,' she said, 'when they should be looking out for the good of the children.'"

Pa looked at Ben. "From the minute you was born, Lucy turned all her teaching energy to you. Though most mamas jabber baby talk at their little ones, she spoke like you was a tiny scholar all wrapped in swaddling clothes. I'll never forget one evening in particular. I'd just hauled in an armful of wood, and she was standing by the window holding you in her arms. She pointed at the sky and said, 'Master Benjamin J. Ward, may I introduce you to the moon?' And she went on to give you a regular astronomy lesson. I didn't understand half of what she was saying, but you smiled like you were soaking in every word."

This was the sort of story that Ben had been begging Pa to tell. Could his mother be the reason Ben had always enjoyed looking at the night sky?

"Later that same week Lucy took sick." Pa's shoulders

sagged as he finished rinsing himself off. "I wanted to fetch the doc, but she said we couldn't afford it." Pa's right hand suddenly gripped the side of the tub so hard that his knuckles turned white. "I shouldn't have listened. By the time I rode to town, it was too late."

"There was no way you could have known," Ben said.

"I should have gone sooner." Pa's voice switched back to his head-cook tone, and he toweled off and dressed without another word.

After Pa left, Ben and Nevers flipped to see who got seconds in the washtub, and Ben won.

While Ben washed up, Nevers said, "It sounds like your mother was a mighty fine lady."

"You know as much about her as I do."

"That's not true."

"Pa never talks like he did just now. I've got to put together bits of stories that I hear from other folks."

"You know lots more than you realize."

"What do you mean?" Ben frowned.

"You're her son, ain't you? Half of what you are came direct from your ma. You already know a heap more about her than any ole story could tell you."

"So maybe I need to be looking for my answers a little closer to home?"

"You learn fast for a Minnesota boy." Nevers tossed a towel to Ben. "And you'd better get out of that tub before icicles start forming in my bathwater."

Love and Lemon Pie

On New Year's Eve Ben got another letter. Nevers was excited when he saw the envelope. "Is that from the boardinghouse lady?" Ben nodded as he drew out a full page of Mrs. Wilson's perfect handwriting.

"Hurry up an' read it," Nevers said.

Dear Benjamin,

Happy New Year!

I hope that things are going well at the lumber camp. Flocks of little chickadees are visiting the bird feeder that you and your friend Nevers sent to me. I know that they appreciate your thoughtfulness as much as I do.

Winter has been uneventful here in Blackwater except for the occasional misfortune suffered by the poor lumberjacks. Another jack turned up dead yesterday. Maggie Montgomery once again had the bad luck to discover the body. She walked down the riverbank to the town water hole and bent to dip her bucket. The body, which had apparently been shoved out under the ice, bobbed right up in Maggie's face.

Poor Maggie ran shrieking all the way to our house. I tried to tease her by telling her that if she's going to keep stumbling across corpses, she may as well apply for the county coroner's job, but she seems to have lost her sense of humor. Maggie is still having heart palpitations, so I will bring her some soup this afternoon to help calm her down.

At least the jack wasn't decapitated like that sad soul they found floating in the river last spring.

Give my best to your father, and remember to say your prayers.

God bless,

Mrs. E. Wilson

P.S. That clumsy Harley just spilled stove blacking all over himself. As if I don't have enough laundry to do. I miss you, Ben.

"What's *decapitated*?" Nevers asked.

"Means your head's been chopped off."

Nevers whistled. "Mrs. Wilson sure can tell a story. I wouldn'ta minded learning to read if our dusty ole school-books had been half that interesting."

Later Ben shared Mrs. Wilson's letter with Charlie,

and he had a good chuckle. "Very amusing again," Charlie said. "Has Mrs. Wilson been a widow for long time?"

"As long as I can recall," Ben said. "Why do you ask?"

"Just wondering. Make sure you tell her how much I admired her letter."

o o o

As a holiday surprise on New Year's Day, Ben and Nevers asked Pa, "How about if we make special dessert for the men?"

"Hash don't qualify as dessert," Pa said.

"We know," Nevers said.

Ben had been talking to Charlie about the foods he missed most from England, and he'd mentioned a special treat called scones. His favorite flavor was black treacle. When he told Ben what was in the recipe, Ben found out that *treacle* was just another word for molasses. "And it doesn't take any more than five minutes to mix up a batch," Charlie said.

"That's the kind of cooking we like," Ben said.

So when the jacks sat down for their New Year's dinner, Ben and Nevers served up Charlie's black treacle scones for dessert (though after considering Charlie's reputation, the boys agreed it was best not to say where they'd gotten the recipe).

"So this is your concoction, eh?" Pa picked up one of the scones and eyed it suspiciously. "Looks kinda like a cross between a biscuit and a cookie."

"I don't care what they look like," said Packy, who was

already finishing his second warm scone. "They're mighty tasty."

"You're supposed to put jam on top," Ben said.

"They don't need no jam," Packy said, cramming a third into his mouth.

The rest of the jacks, Pa included, agreed with Packy, and they soon polished off all two hundred scones. Slim even walked up and shook Ben's and Nevers's hands. "Fine baking, boys," he said, giving them good reason to stand taller.

Ben brought some scones to the dentist's shack, and Charlie closed his eyes and smiled when he took his first bite. "The smell of warm treacle takes me right back to the old Tyneside cottage where I was born," he said. "I can see my mum like it was yesterday, humming as she pulled her baking pan out of the oven."

Later, as the boys were cleaning up the dishes, Ben said, "I thought two hundred scones would be way too many."

"Jacks can never have too much of a good thing," Pa said. "Seeing those fellows smile reminds me of how a recipe helped me win your mother's hand."

"Really?" Ben said.

Pa nodded. "I never thought I had a chance with Lucy Warren. She was being courted by every fellow in Itasca and Koochiching County. There were bankers and lumbermen and rich farmers calling on her all the time. A man who had a stake in a gold mine up by Rainy Lake even asked for her hand. But it was a pie that won her over."

Nevers and Ben both frowned.

"I'm not pulling your legs, boys. After I was discharged from the army down in St. Louis, I traveled around and tried lots of jobs. Went as far west as Nevada. I finally headed north when I heard there were cooking jobs in the Blackwater Valley. My first summer in town I watched a parade of gentlemen callers stopping by the house where Lucy was boarding. I figured I didn't have a chance, but she was such a pretty gal that I couldn't help stopping by, and I brought along a lemon meringue pie.

"We sat on the porch and visited a long while. She asked me where I'd lived and what I did during the war. Most gals don't care to hear war stories, but she was impressed at how we'd volunteered our battlefield kitchen for a hospital when the docs had nowhere else to set up— a meat saw works just as good on a soldier's leg as it does on a soup bone." Pa stopped when he saw Nevers turning pale. "Sorry, boy. I only bring it up 'cause Lucy appreciated that I'd had experiences beyond this little valley. She especially liked hearing about my silver prospecting days."

"You were a silver miner?" Ben asked.

"I guess I never told you about that, did I?"

Ben shook his head, wondering what else Pa hadn't told him.

"Though Lucy and I had a nice talk," Pa continued, "I was sure that my being older than the rest of the fellows who'd come courting put me at a disadvantage. But she surprised me by saying, 'With all the young colts who have been cavorting around here, I'd forgotten how much

I appreciate the company of a mature man. Most importantly, I can tell you know how to treat a woman.'

" 'How's that?' I asked.

" 'You never even saw Nell walk by, did you?'

" 'Did Miss Nell pass?' I asked.

" 'She comes this way every afternoon. All the fellows study her real close, but you had your eyes on me instead.'

"But in the end," Pa said, "I'm convinced it was the pie that did the trick. After one bite she smiled and said, 'You certainly know how to turn a girl's head, Jack Ward. Not only are you tall, dark, and handsome, but you also bake a mighty fine pie.'

"We were married the next spring."

"You figure these scones are good enough to get me a girl someday, Mr. Ward?" Nevers asked.

"Hard to tell," Pa said, "but in my experience ladies are partial to pie."

Ben smiled. Now that Pa had shared another story about Mother, maybe he'd be willing to tell some more.

Later, as they were climbing into their bunks, Ben got to thinking about what Pa had said about the war. If he'd seen shot-up soldiers lying right in his kitchen, that might explain what Mrs. Wilson had said about him carrying the weight of the world on his shoulders.

"Was the war hard, Pa?" Ben asked.

Pa waited until Nevers had settled under his blankets before he spoke. "You'd think being a cook wouldn't be so bad." Pa's voice was soft in the dark. "But there's nothing harder than feeding fellows when you know they're going off to die. Eat and die. That's all it was. Those boys—some no older than you and Nevers—were nothing but cannon fodder. I did my best to give 'em good food and cheer. But even as I ladled up their plates, I knew they'd be coming back all shot to pieces." Pa's voice got even quieter. "It was thirty years ago, but I can see their faces like it was yesterday."

Ben couldn't imagine having to live with the faces of dead soldiers frozen in your mind. That would be like Packy going off to the cut and coming back dead. Ben would be forever seeing him grinning and holding a cookie in each hand.

ONE-PLUG PRINCE AND
THE TOTE-ROAD SHAGAMAW

The day after New Year's a cold front moved in. When Jiggers grumbled about the weather as he got up from breakfast, the push said, "What did you expect? This here is Minnesota, not Floreeda."

"You should lard up your socks like I do," Swede said, finishing off his sixth cup of blackjack. Swede's cure for cold feet was rubbing lard on his toes before he put on his socks.

"I ain't filling my boots with pig fat even if it gets to be a hundred below," Jiggers said.

"Then you should try sprinkling pepper in your boots like I do," Poultice Pete said.

"I ain't peppering or salting my feet, neither," Jiggers said. "I swear, we got us a bunch a lunatics in this camp. Food belongs in a fellow's belly, not his boots."

While Ben and Nevers were picking up the breakfast dishes, a heavy stick of firewood rolled out of the wood box and nearly smashed Nevers's foot, but he danced out of the way.

"What sort of jobs do you get in the summer?" Ben asked as he retrieved the fat chunk of oak.

"I usually hire on at a farm or a livery stable," Nevers said. "Why you asking?"

"Seein' how quick you dodged that stove wood, I bet you'd make a dandy log driver," Ben said.

"You think so? I've always wondered what it'd be like to ride those logs downstream to the mill."

"Me too." Ben smiled.

"You suppose they'd let us sign on this spring?" Nevers grinned. "Imagine runnin' the river all the way to Canada."

"It'd be a lot more fun than mucking out a barn," Ben said.

"You boys cleaning or gabbing?" Pa yelled from the storeroom. "It sounds like a ladies' aid society meetin' out there."

⦿ ⦿ ⦿

Later that week the push finally admitted he was worried about the weather. "I hope it don't get no colder," he said to Pa. "The jacks can stand anything, but if it drops any lower, I'll have to keep in the horses."

That meant a day of hauling would be canceled. Even if the sawyers and skid men kept working, Ben knew that the profits of the company depended on how fast the logs could be landed on the riverbank. The push often said, "A day without hauling is money down the spillway."

Each morning when the push stopped by for his blackjack, he and Pa talked about the cold. It was understood that the kitchen crew would keep the temperature a secret. The push said, "If those jacks knew how cold it was, they'd want every day off all winter long."

On the morning of January second the push had thirty-five below. Even with a scarf wrapped across his face, Ben's eyelashes froze while he was driving the swingdingle. He could hear the runners of the hauling sleds squeaking from two miles away. The friction of the sleds melted away a fraction of an inch from the ice ruts, but they refroze instantly after the load passed.

Like all the teamsters, Ed Day drove his sled standing up. To keep his feet warm he stood on a gunny sack stuffed with hay laid across the front platform. On the coldest mornings Day had to hook a second team ahead of his leaders to break out his runners.

But no matter how cold the weather, Day stayed calm and kept a close eye on his team. While the rest of the fellows ran to the lunch line, Day checked each of his horses before he fed himself.

One afternoon Day was about to start his team when his leader stomped his foot and snorted.

Day said, "Sorry, Prince," and reached into his coat pocket. "I almost forgot your lunch." Day held out a twist of tobacco, and his horse snatched it up.

The horse chewed hungrily as Day walked back to his sleigh. Ben couldn't believe his eyes. He'd seen the jacks get ornery when the pencil pusher ran short of snuff, or snooze, as Swede called his "Norwegian gunpowder," but he'd never heard of a horse that had a tobacco chewing habit.

When Day saw Ben, he said, "I call him Prince Albert 'cause he's got a taste for tobacco. He prefers Peerless, but he'll take a plug of Climax if he has to. I expect he'd smoke a pipe if I lit one for him. Some of the boys call him One-Plug, since he won't pull worth a darn until he gets his daily ration." Day took his wide-legged driving stance and picked up his reins. "I'd normally sell off a finicky animal like him, but I never have seen his equal when it comes to hauling."

Ben grinned as he finished loading the frozen dishes onto the swingdingle. He could imagine Prince puffing on a pipe as he pulled the sled to the landing.

On Sunday afternoon Ben and Nevers headed down to the bunkhouse to visit. The cold spell had been making Pa and the rest of the jacks so crabby that the day before, when Ben had had to go to the clerk's shack, Wally's usual grumpy mood hadn't even bothered him. Ben had asked Wally, "How early in the spring do you hire your log drivers?" but the clerk had only said, "That depends." Ben had also been trying his best to get Pa to tell another story about his mother, but Pa was back to his old silent self.

"How can it be so sunny and still be cold?" Nevers asked as he hunkered down in his mackinaw on their way to the bunkhouse.

When Ben stepped into the bunkhouse, the hot smell of the stove mingled with woodsmoke and wet wool.

"Hang your caps and mitts on the line, boys," Windy said.

"I lost one of the wool liners for my mitts," Nevers said.

"You must've been robbed by a tote-road shagamaw."

"What's that?" Nevers asked.

"Haven't you ever heard of a shagamaw?"

Ben and Nevers both shook their heads.

"Any time you lose something made out of wool—a hat, mitten, or even a mackinaw—that means a tote-road shagamaw has snatched it up. Wool is their main diet, but you never see one 'cause they're so shy. They have bear paws in front and moose hooves in back, and they switch from one set to the other so often you can't track them down."

Ben knew Windy was teasing, but Nevers said, "Really?"

"A buddy of mine back in Michigan was following some moose tracks one day. All of a sudden the tracks changed to bear prints. He stopped and scratched his head. The tracks kept switching from moose to bear every quarter mile. Then they turned due north at a witness tree. Not only was that shagamaw following the section lines, he was changing his walking style every quarter mile. He'd been following timber cruisers and had copied their style of pacing out square sections of timber. But being that the shagamaw is low on brainpower, he could only count as high as four hundred and forty steps before he had to start over."

Ben looked at the other fellows. There wasn't a hint of doubt on any of their faces. In fact, Windy's talk of hungry wool-eating critters caused several men to check the clothesline to make sure all their things were there.

When Ben and Nevers walked back to the cookshack,

it was even colder than before. "It feels like winter ain't never gonna end," Nevers said.

"It'll be worth the wait when spring comes and we're riding a stick of pine down a white-water rapids."

"Only if the push and that crazy clerk'll sign us on."

"They will," Ben said.

"And if your pa lets you go."

"I'll work on him when the time comes," Ben said, hoping that his bold talk would actually come true.

WEATHER BOY

"**D**oggone it, Jack," the push said as he sat down for his midmorning cup of blackjack the next day, "I wish thermometers had never been invented."

"What'd she read this morning?" Pa asked.

"Twenty-nine below. And by the look of that clear sky, we're headed for colder."

Ben couldn't help asking, "What good is it to hate thermometers? It's gonna get just as cold whether you know the temperature or not."

Pa and Nevers turned and stared. The minute Ben saw their faces, he knew he was in trouble. When was he going to learn to stop blurting things out?

"You keep your nose—" Pa started.

"That's all right, Jack," the push said. "I like a boy who speaks his mind. If this cookee likes thermometers so much, maybe we should make him our weather boy."

"That would serve him right," Pa said.

"What's a weather boy?" Ben asked.

"Before you start your morning cooking, you can check the temperature for me," the push said. Ben wished he'd kept his mouth shut. "Can I show our weather boy my thermometer?"

"Be my guest," Pa said, nodding.

The push walked to the clerk's shack with Ben trailing behind. The pencil pusher smirked as the push reached into a trunk beside his bunk and pulled out a black case. "You keep this hid"—he handed it to Ben—"except when you take it outside in the morning. Don't you ever let those jacks know the temperature or I'll skin your hide."

"Wake up, weather boy," Pa said the next morning, instead of "Daylight in the swamp." Ben yawned as he slipped on his pants. It was only twenty minutes earlier than he normally got up, but it felt like an hour. Nevers was still snoring in the next bunk.

Following the push's directions, Ben took the thermometer and its metal stand out of the black case he'd stashed under his bunk. Then he pulled on his boots and shirt. "Happy temperature taking," Pa said as Ben stepped outside.

Woodsmoke trailed off the cookshack roof. Ben's boots squeaked on the hard-packed snow, and his nose burned in the cold. As the air rushed down his back, he wished he'd put on his hat along with his mackinaw. Squinting under the blue points of starlight, he checked his pocket watch. The push had told him to set the thermometer in the open and wait five minutes before he took his reading. Ben stomped his feet and looked up. He'd always enjoyed gazing at the stars. Now that Pa had told him the story about his mother cradling him under a full moon, he connected his love of the night sky to her. It fit Nevers's theory about Ben's having things in common with his mother. When the five minutes was up, Ben's toes were numb. He struck a match and crouched down. It was thirty-six below.

As soon as the push arrived for breakfast, he stepped into the kitchen and lowered his voice. "You got some news for me, cookee?" He looked to make sure no one was listening.

Ben told him the temperature, and he nodded. "That's plenty warm for highball logging."

When it came time for Ben to drive the swingdingle, he could understand the push's policy of keeping the temperature a secret. The whole way to the cut, all Ben could think of was the cold. The air burned his cheeks right through his scarf, and his eyelashes iced up so badly that he had to squint to see.

"This weather ain't fit for man nor beast," Packy said. Ben could tell Packy was about to complain more until he saw that Old Dan was frosted from his whiskers to his tail. "Would you look at that poor hoss? I'll blanket him while you get the lunch ready."

Everyone but Swede ate with his mitts on. No matter how close the jacks huddled to the fire or how quickly they spooned down their food, nobody could clean his plate before the last beans froze solid. "Listen!" Jiggers said, pounding on a frozen clump. "It sounds like I'm banging on metal."

"Nobody should have to work in weather like this," Packy said. "All you do is break chains and smash your fingers. A fellow—"

"A fellow should keep his trap shut," Swede said. "You ladies might as well start a sewing circle."

Ignoring Swede, Day said, "Would you boys mind helping me break out my load?"

Packy and Jiggers got up. Then Day turned to Ben. "Would the cookee trade his ladle for a maul?"

"Sure," Ben said.

Packy and Jiggers hooked their skidding horses ahead of Day's leaders as a snatch team. Day handed a pry bar to the road monkey and a heavy maul to Ben. "You give the runners a whack while the monkey pries them forward."

Day took his driving stance. "Ready?"

"Anytime," Packy said.

"Ho, boys," Day spoke to his team. "Let's walk."

As Day's Percherons pulled, the snatch team jerked hard to the right. Ben pounded on the left runner while the road monkey pried from the rear. "Switch," Day called, and while the team pulled to the left, Ben and the road monkey ran around and worked on the opposite runner.

It took two jerks on each side before the runners broke free. With a shuddering creak the sled started forward. Packy and Jiggers kept their horses pulling for the first fifty yards. Then they stepped aside.

The ice ruts were so cold that Ben could hear Day's runners squeaking the whole time he loaded his dishes. On the way back to the cookshack Ben had to fight a sharp north wind. He got so cold that he could barely pry his hands loose from the reins and climb down from the swingdingle.

When Ben opened the cookshack door, he heard laughing. He figured it was Windy, but it was Pa slapping his knee and chuckling.

Pa and Nevers didn't even notice Ben until they felt the cold from the door. "You back already?" Pa said.

"I was just telling your pa about a fellow who owned a roadhouse restaurant back home, and he got caught selling barbecued groundhog as pork ribs."

"That must have been a *rib* tickler when the folks found out." Pa laughed at his own joke.

Ben tried to smile. If only Pa would kid around with him like that.

Nevers said, "You look froze solid. Let me help you carry the dishes in."

They unloaded quickly. Nevers dumped the plates into the dishpan, saying, "We've got a heap of scraping to do."

Ben put on his apron and picked up a plate. "How much colder can it get?"

"A fellow in my last camp claimed it's always the coldest in the low areas," Nevers said, scraping a stubborn clump of beans.

"Like right in this valley," Ben said. He poured boiling water into the dishpan, and steam rose, making his frozen cheeks tingle.

Nevers nodded. "Yep. We're in prime country for record-setting cold."

The next morning Ben was glad to see that it had warmed up to twenty-two below. When Ben took Charlie his breakfast, the dentist noticed Ben's face the minute he stepped inside the shack.

"Why the hangdog look?" Charlie asked.

"What do you mean?" Ben asked.

"You look like you just lost your best mate."

"It's nothing."

"If that's the sort of face you make over nothing, I'd hate to see you sad."

Ben set down the lunch. "All Pa does is holler at me."

"Let me tell you something about fathers." Charlie laid his file on the table. "Your pa's job is to toughen you up so you're ready for anything life throws your way. My father never coddled me. He worked as a longshoreman, loading cargo from the time he was thirteen until the day he busted his back forty years later. Your pa's too busy to be preening your feathers."

Just then Pa yelled, "Bennn . . ."

That afternoon Windy stopped by the cookshack and said, "Ernie Gunderson's real sick. He's been clutching his stomach and groaning since breakfast."

Pa glared at Ben. "Don't look at me, Pa. Nevers and I have been washing our hands twenty times every day."

144

"The push figures it's appendicitis," Windy said. "He's sending him to town with the tote teamster."

When the tote teamster arrived, Ben and Nevers unloaded the supplies, and then they helped Gundy into the back of the sleigh. "Thanks," Gundy said in a weak voice. He groaned as he lay down in the straw of the wagon bed, and Ben covered him with a blanket.

Windy walked over to the teamster and whispered something. The teamster grinned and spoke in a loud voice: "You got an ax handle, Windy?"

"What for?" Windy asked.

"I just need it for a minute," the teamster said. "I can't stand fellows being in pain. I'm gonna crack this boy on the noggin so he'll rest easy while I'm driving back to town."

"What if you hit him too hard?" Windy asked.

"We'll just have to fit him for a coffin, then." The teamster picked up the ax handle and walked back toward the sleigh. "But that don't happen very often."

The minute the teamster put his hand on the side of the sleigh box, Gundy sat up. "I'm feeling better," he said.

The teamster laughed. "We figured you had a bad case of blanket fever. If you're just riding back to town to see that gal of yours, you might as well sit up front with me."

FELLED BY A BLUE BUTT

The men had just returned from the cut when Ed
Day walked into the cookshack. His face was
pale. "Slim Cantwell was finishing off a load
when the cross hauler's horse slipped on a patch of ice."
He stopped and lowered his eyes. "Slim never had a
chance. The top log took his stems out from under him
and crushed him flat."

Ben nearly dropped a gallon can of prunes on the
floor. Not Slim! Not Slim, the surefooted loader. He could
cap off a sled with a two-ton stick of pine and keep his
pipe lit the whole time!

Poultice Pete stood listening at the door. "Warn't
nothin' nobody could do. We hustled up to the top and
hooked that log offa him, but it was too late."

Ben was numb as the rest of the lumberjacks filed in
for supper with their heads down. Even Swede, who never
complimented anyone but himself, said, "There weren't a
finer man in the woods than Cantwell."

"He was the best I ever saw," the push agreed, nodding. He sighed. "We put his body in the root cellar to

cool. Now I got to write to Slim's widow and her seven little ones at home."

Everyone had a respectful attitude except Jiggers, who walked up to the push and said, "If you'll be needing a new top loader, I'd be willing to take the job."

Ben couldn't believe that Jiggers would be worried about a promotion at a time like this. That was like trying to pick Slim's pocket at his funeral.

As the jacks were finishing their supper, Pa picked up an empty pitcher. "Why don't you fetch us some molasses, Ben. I'd like you and Nevers to teach me your scone recipe tomorrow."

"But—" Ben swallowed at the thought of the body in the root cellar.

"Don't go worrying about Slim," Pa said. "The poor fellow is doornail dead. The boys held a mirror under his nose and even poked him with a pin to make sure he was past helping. Here." He tossed the pitcher to Ben.

Nevers looked grateful that Pa hadn't picked him for the job, but Pa said, "You might as well go along, Nevers, and bring us back a bushel of spuds."

Ben lit a lantern and crept out the back door with Nevers at his side. "That cellar gives me the creeps on a sunny day," Nevers said, "and now we gotta go down there in the dark with— It makes my skin all crawly."

"There's nothing to be afraid of." Ben talked braver than he felt. As he swung the door open, a puff of wind blew out his lantern. When he knelt to relight the wick, Nevers said, "How come your fingers are shaking?"

With the lantern casting flickering shadows on the walls, Ben led the way down the steps. As his boot touched the dirt floor, Ben expected to see Slim's pale face, but to his relief, the body was covered with a blanket. Ben took a breath and hung his lantern on a nail. He tiptoed to the molasses barrel and opened the spigot, while Nevers walked to the potato bin. Ben was wishing the pitcher would fill faster when he heard a whisper.

"What'd you say?" Ben asked, bending down to shut the spigot.

"I didn't say nothing," Nevers said.

The hair on Ben's neck prickled. The muffled voice came again. "I'm cold."

Ben whirled. Slim sat up with the blanket covering his face. Ben dropped the pitcher and screamed. Nevers bolted for the steps with Ben right behind him. They fell twice scrambling up the stairs, and ran to the cookshack. Nevers almost ripped the door off the hinges as he burst inside. "It's alive!" he yelled. "Slim's alive down there in—"

The jacks stared at him. "Are you deaf?" Ben said, feeling like he was going crazy. Just then the door opened behind him.

It was Slim, smoking his pipe and holding the pitcher in his hand. "I believe you dropped this, son," he said.

Then the men all roared at once. Ben looked at Pa. He and Jiggers were standing side by side, and Pa was slapping him on the shoulder. They'd all been in on the trick.

In the morning Ben was glad to see that the jacks had forgotten the joke. They filed into the cookshack, took their seats, and started shoveling down food.

When Ed Day raised an empty platter, Ben walked toward the table. "Hey, cookee. Is it true that you and Nevers are leaving camp and enrolling in undertaker's school?"

Everyone laughed, and Pa hooted just as loudly as the rest of the jacks.

After the men left, Ben said to Nevers, "We can't get riled over the teasing."

"That's for sure," Nevers said. "A jack in my last camp wouldn't take his medicine after they played a joke on him. The more he complained, the more they picked on him."

"Unless we want to be called undertakers for the rest of our lives, we'd best laugh along."

"And being teased beats chopping cotton any day."

"Is chopping how you harvest the cotton?" Ben asked.

"No." Nevers laughed. "It's how you weed it. After my daddy left us, me and Mama tried to sharecrop on our own. I was only ten at the time, but I could chop cotton just fine and walk a passable furrow behind a plow. The landowner advanced us seed and fertilizer, and we promised to give him half our corn and cotton crops—we could keep all the taters—come harvesttime. After a hot summer of sweat and hope and weeding, it looked like we were gonna make it. That's when Mama took sick. Working as a cropper was a church picnic compared to being throwed in an orphanage."

"Weren't there any other relatives to take you in?"

"Mama's kin were all dead, and the folks on Daddy's side cut me off cold just like he done."

"I guess I should be grateful for Mrs. Wilson."

"Count your lucky stars that you had your pa and a nice lady to look after you."

THE COLDEST DAY

A warm spell brought relief in mid January. But when Ben asked if he could quit taking the temperature, the push said, "You best keep after it. Even March can get cold up here."

That meant Ben would have get up early for two more months! Why had he gone and talked to the push about hating thermometers?

The cold returned on January twenty-fourth, and for the next eighteen days it never got above zero, even during the day. When Ben recorded thirty-two below on the twenty-eighth, the push said, "If it's colder than forty below tomorrow, you'd best wake me so we can hold the horses back."

The next morning it was forty-eight below. Ben tried to be quiet as he crept into the clerk's office to wake the push, but as soon as the door creaked, he heard a pistol cock. A voice said, "Identificate yourself or die."

Ben had forgotten that the pencil pusher kept a loaded pistol under his pillow. Ben was ready to dive for the floor when the push spoke up. "It's all right, Wally.

The cookee's bringing me a weather report. What's the verdict?"

"Forty-eight below."

The push was surprisingly calm. He swung his feet to the floor and said, "I'll go tell Needlenose and Day myself."

The cold weather made the men extra grumpy again. Keeping the horses in meant that the teamsters had to help with the felling. And since Dan couldn't haul the swingdingle out to the cut, the men had to walk a mile and a half back for lunch. "I feel like a green road monkey having to hoof all the way in for my beans," Packy grumbled.

The next morning, even with his mackinaw buttoned up to his chin and his hat pulled down over his ears, the five minutes it took Ben to get a temperature reading left him shaking. Fifty-one below. When he delivered the news, the push yelled, "How's a fellow gonna get any wood put up in this doggone country?"

The jacks went back to work the following day, but on February ninth Ben had to wake the push and tell him that it was the coldest day of the winter—fifty-eight below.

"Dagnabit, cookee." The push kicked a chair against the wall. "What kinda news is that?" Ben wasn't sure if the push was more angry at the weather or at his hurt foot. He limped back to the bunk and rubbed his toes. "Go tell Windy and Day that we got to keep the men in along with the horses."

Everyone enjoyed having the day off except Swede, who growled, "Are we lumberjacks or grandmothers?"

The cookshack had burned so much firewood overnight that Ben and Nevers had to make a trip to the woodpile after breakfast. When they stepped out back, the snow crunched under Nevers's boots with a high-pitched squeak. "Would you listen to that!" Nevers said. He waved for Ben to stop and walked a few steps ahead.

Ben said, "I've never heard snow that loud." The air was so cold that his eyes felt prickly and his lungs burned. When he stooped to gather an armload of split birch, he spit into a snowbank. To his surprise, his spit crackled and froze in the air.

"Did you hear that?" Nevers said.

Ben nodded. "This has got to be the coldest day ever."

"I'll say," Nevers said, laughing as his own spit froze in midair. The boys spit again and again, giggling at the crackling.

Just then Pa opened the door. "What in the Sam Hill is goin' on out here! I thought I asked you boys to fetch some wood."

Ben and Nevers stopped laughing.

Pa looked at Ben meanly; then he smiled.

"What's wrong?" Ben asked.

Nevers said, "You got a spit icicle hanging from your chin."

Ben wiped his chin with the back of his mitt, but he missed. "Over there." Nevers pointed, but Ben missed the icicle again. Suddenly everyone was laughing together.

"I only seen it this cold once before." Pa stopped to catch his breath. "Let me show you something."

He went back inside and came out with a pan of steaming tea. He had a dipper in his hand. "Watch this," he said. Scooping up a dipperful of tea, he flung it into the air. Ben was ready to cover up his head, but the tea turned to ice crystals and floated gently to the ground.

Nevers said, "Can we try?"

Pa nodded.

Nevers handed the dipper to Ben. "You go first." Ben tossed a ladleful up and watched it turn to instant frost flakes. The three of them oohed and aahed like they were watching a fireworks display.

Nevers stepped a few paces away and tossed some tea at Ben, but the push came around the corner just as Nevers let loose. The half-frozen tea spattered onto his face.

Everyone stopped laughing. The push looked mad at first. Then he smiled at Pa. "What's this, Jack? Some new recipe?"

"Want to try, sir?" Nevers said, holding out the dipper.

After looking over his shoulder to see if anyone else was watching, the push said, "Don't mind if I do." With a grin he bent down and scooped up some hot tea.

SNOW SNAKES AND HODAGS

After the lunch dishes were done, Ben and Nevers walked down to the bunkhouse for a visit. Even with the sun full in the sky, the cold stung Ben's cheeks.

Nevers scrunched the snow under his boots. "I don't care if it gets down to sixty below if we get double Sundays out of it."

"Two days off in one week!" Ben said. "Even if we have to cook, not hauling those frozen dishes back from the cut saves us a heap of boiling and scraping."

Just before they got to the bunkhouse, Ben said, "I think I figured a way to get back at those jacks for tricking us."

"What you got in mind?"

"Let's visit the pencil pusher."

Wally scoffed when he saw the boys. "I suppose both of you gazebos went and cut yourselves this time."

"Nope," Ben said.

"Did you come to bother me about hiring on as log drivers?"

"Not that, neither," Ben said. "I need a bottle of castor oil."

The pencil pusher grinned meanly. "Got the bloats, eh?"

"I been feeling poorly."

Wally picked a greasy-looking green bottle off his shelf and plunked it on the counter. "This will get you trotting to the outhouse before you can whistle 'Dixie.'"

When Wally started to write down the cost of the castor oil in his ledger, Nevers said, "You can charge half to me."

"You bound up, too?"

Nevers nodded and made a pained face. But the minute they got outside, he grinned. "Are you planning what I think you are?"

"The only way to get back at those jacks is through their stomachs," Ben said. "And as strong as Pa seasons up his beans, I figure no one will notice if we stir in a little castor oil."

"For good measure I'll borrow a board from the wood butcher and nail the outhouse door shut when we spring the trick."

"We'll teach them to scare us." Ben chuckled. "I'll stash this bottle in the cookshack."

"See you in the bunkhouse," Nevers said.

On his way to the bunkhouse Ben swung by the filer's shack. At first Charlie only talked about how hard it was going to be for the company to fill its contract if the weather stayed bad. Then Ben looked up at his mother's photograph. "Do you know where that was took? I don't have a single picture of my mother."

Charlie put down his file and rubbed his eyes. "I'll be straight, lad. I've told you every detail I can about Lucinda Warren. You've got to remember that as smitten as I was, I only spent a few months with her. Your father knew her for years."

"For a while I thought Pa was gonna talk more, but he's barely said a thing lately."

"The bigger the hurt, the longer it takes to heal."

"You're the same as Pa," Ben said, his voice rising more than he'd planned. "You want to keep everything to yourself."

Charlie looked at Ben, but he didn't say anything.

"The trouble with you is you've been hiding in the woods too long. You're like that Thoreau fellow who went to Walden Pond. Only difference is you never came back."

Ben slammed the door behind him. Not caring which direction he went, Ben marched past the blacksmith's shop and down the road. But the cold air brought him to his senses. Why had he yelled at Charlie? It wasn't Charlie's fault that Ben's mother had died so young. How could he have been so stupid? Ben kicked an ice chunk, and it flew into a clump of frozen hazel brush. Feeling foolish, he covered his ears with his hands and jogged back to camp.

When he stepped into the bunkhouse, Windy yelled, "Close that door, you gazebo. I've burned up two days' worth of wood already." The card players cussed him for letting in a draft.

Ben took a seat by Nevers, who asked, "What took you so long? You look froze."

"I went for a little walk."

"In this weather? You must be getting as batty as that old dentist." Nevers went back to watching the card game.

The top of the stove and the first joint of the chimney pipe were cherry red, and the draft plate rattled from the rush of air. The lower logs on every wall were covered with a thick coating of white frost. Poultice Pete had both his mackinaw and hat on. "You might as well turn those earflaps down, too, you big sissy," Swede said to him.

"Don't mind if I do," Pete said. Laying his cards on the table, he pulled his flaps over both ears.

"Hold up the game, why don't you!" Swede shouted. "In all my days I have never seen such a pack of lily-livered lumberjacks."

Packy finally spoke up. "If you're so set on proving your stupidity, why don't you take your Swedish fiddle out to the cut and drop a pine on that thick skull of yours?"

"His fiddle?" Nevers looked at Ben.

"His saw."

"Don't you call me a thick skull," Swede said, looking down at Packy's feet. "You're the one that don't have brains enough to wear boots in the wintertime."

Packy had to laugh at that, and the tension eased. Ben looked under the table. Though Packy was barefooted as usual, he was keeping his feet off the floor by resting his heels on the bottom rung of the chair.

Without looking up from his whittling, Windy asked Nevers, "What does our Carolina boy think of Minnesota winters now?"

"Ben and I decided it's boot-squeaking cold," Nevers said.

"I'll bet you miss home in weather like this."

"Maybe a smidgin." Nevers cracked his knuckles as he talked. "But once my ma died, I couldn't get shed of that place fast enough. It might be warm in Carolina, but the nice weather breeds a heap of ornery critters. And I don't just mean gallinippers like you got around here."

"Gallinippers?" Ben asked.

"That's what we call mosquitoes. But they're nothing compared to the copperheads and rattlesnakes and biting spiders."

"We got our share of snakes around here, too," Jiggers said.

"Would you play cards!" Swede yelled.

"What's he mean?" Nevers asked.

"Jiggers is talking about snow snakes," Windy said.

"Snow snakes?"

"The cold don't bother them because they travel under the snow," Windy said. "On a day like today they burrow deep under the drifts and hide."

Nevers's eyes got big.

"That's why you got to be on the lookout when you bend down to pick something up out of the snow. They'll grab your throat quicker than you can blink," Windy said. "And we got other animals you haven't heard of."

"Like what?"

"Like the hodag. It's about the size of a small steer. Though it moves slow, it's as smart as a whip. It's got a hairless body covered in a striped and checked pattern like the mackinaw coats the jacks wear—that's why they're so blamed hard to see in the woods. Instead of a horn, the hodag has a large, spade-shaped bone that blocks his vision. Being that he can only look up, his main diet is porcupine. He meanders through the woods, peering into treetops. Whenever he spots a porky, he blinks his eyes and licks his chops. Then he probes the ground with his spade bone. Once the roots are loose, he steps back and rams the tree with his head. As soon as it topples over, he straddles the trunk and walks along it until he finds the stunned porky, which he swallows headfirst."

"How do they live in the winter?" Nevers asked.

"When fall comes, they rub against a big ole balsam and cover up with pitch. They roll around in a patch of hardwood, coat theirselves with leaves, and lie down and nap till spring."

"If only you jabbermouths would do the same," Swede said.

A Soggy Outfit

The following morning, when it came time to deliver breakfast, Ben dreaded facing Charlie. He turned to Nevers and said, "Would you like to take a turn at bringin'—"

"Stop right there," Nevers interrupted him.

On his way to Charlie's, Ben watched a raven flying over the bunkhouse, holding a branch in her claws. That meant she was already building her nest, and despite the cold, spring would be coming soon.

Ben thought about rapping on the door and leaving Charlie's tray on the steps. But he knew he'd have to face him sooner or later. When Ben knocked on the door, his knuckles hurt from the cold, and he wished he'd worn choppers.

"Come in," Charlie said.

Ben stepped inside and, avoiding Charlie's eyes, set the tray on the table.

Charlie saved him by asking, "Is it still a little nippy?"

"It was twenty-nine below by my—" Ben stopped. "I'm not supposed to tell anyone I've been reading the push's thermometer."

"We can keep it our secret," Charlie said. "The exact temperature doesn't matter to me. I can gauge how much set these misery whips need by eyeing the frost on the windowpane."

"Charlie," Ben began. "I'm sorry for spouting off like I did."

"There's no need to apologize, squire."

"I know you've told me all you can about my mother. I just feel like a big chunk of my life is missing. I never even knew what she looked like till I saw your photograph."

"You don't have a picture of your own mum?" Charlie asked.

"Pa's only photograph is all blurry and water stained."

"It's natural for you to grab on to every little fragment."

"But I shouldn't have yelled at you."

"I had it coming. I've been thinking about what Lucinda would've thought of a fellow who ran off and hid in the woods like I have. Remember how your mother thought that Thoreau made the proper choice in leaving Walden Pond?" Charlie paused and looked at the window again. "You're right to say I've put in a whole lot more time in the woods than Thoreau ever did."

"So what'll you do?" Ben asked.

"For now I'm going to eat some breakfast and file some more misery whips."

"And after that?"

"There'll be lots more saw blades and breakfasts coming my way."

The next day Ben and Nevers decided to play their trick during breakfast. Nevers distracted Pa by asking, "How do you know the right amount of starter for those sourdough flapjacks of yours?"

While Pa was explaining the finer points of his sweat pad recipe, Ben poured the castor oil into the beans. He had planned to stop at half a bottle, but since Pa was so busy with his flapjack lecture, he decided to empty the whole thing.

When the fellows sat down to eat, Ben was worried that they might notice a funny taste to the beans. Though a few of the jacks frowned, they dug right in and cleaned their plates as usual. Meanwhile, Nevers slipped out the back door.

"What's that pounding outside?" Packy asked when he heard Nevers nailing on the outhouse.

"Must be woodpeckers," Swede said.

As the men were drinking their last cups of swamp water, Ben heard some stomachs rumbling. Then, as the mixture took effect, a few of the jacks started to shift nervously on their benches.

"Would you fellows like to add a little more flavor to your beans?" Ben asked, holding up the empty castor oil bottle.

Packy shouted something in French, and he jumped up and ran out the door with a dozen fellows trailing behind. Ben could tell when Packy reached the outhouse door because he yelled again, twice as loudly. Pa walked outside to see what was going on.

Nevers came back looking pale. "Do you suppose they're gonna kill us?"

"Is it bad?" Ben asked.

"There must be twenty fellows at the edge of the woods with their pants dropped."

What seemed like a long while later, Packy dragged himself back to the door of the cookshack. Pa was with him. Ben was glad to see that Packy didn't have an ax in his hand. "The boys have been talking," the Frenchman started. "They all thought that you'd crossed the line with that little stunt, but then I reminded them that they'd crossed it first with that dead body trick."

"They ain't mad, then?"

"Oh, they're plenty mad, but they figure things are even now."

Pa was not so kind. "Don't never forget you got lucky this time, boys. And if you ever mess with my cooking again, I'll send you both down the road."

○ ● ○

By week's end the weather had warmed so much that water was dripping off the cookshack roof. After breakfast on Friday, Pa sent Ben to the clerk's shack with an order. "By the look of those icicles, spring can't be far off," Ben said.

"Maybe, maybe not," Wally said. "I've seen it snow up here on the Fourth of July."

"I suppose the thaw means you'll be hiring log drivers soon."

"We gotta get the timber out of the woods before we can worry about driving it to the mill." Wally turned his attention to his ledger book.

Later that same morning, when the push was finishing his blackjack, Ben said, "Isn't this warm weather nice?"

"Are you nuts?" the push said. "If it ain't too cold in this place, it's too hot. I swear that purgatory would be an improvement after spending a lifetime logging in Minnesota." He banged down his cup and marched out the door.

"What's wrong with him?" Ben asked.

"The sleds'll bust through the ruts if it gets too warm," Pa said.

"I can recall losing the roads twice myself," Windy added. "Both times the company couldn't fill their contract, and the crews never got paid. I figure one bad season wouldn't bust these folks, but you never can tell."

When the temperature stayed above freezing for three days in a row, the push took Day aside after breakfast. "You set to switch to night hauling?"

"I warned the boys to be ready," Day said.

The next day the teamsters napped in the bunkhouse through the afternoon and didn't start running their teams until the rest of the fellows had gone to bed. Day finished his last load just before breakfast, and he beat Packy to the cookshack for the first time all year.

"How did it go?" Pa asked as he hung up the Gabriel horn.

"The road's holding," Day said, "but if the water tank crew can't ice the ruts, we'll lose her pretty quick."

The jacks came in from the woods, looking just as tired as Day. "Way the water's dripping off the trees," Jiggers said, "we might as well be working in a rainstorm. That bunkhouse is beginning to smell like rotten pond scum."

"What's the use in bothering to hang up our britches at night when they can't even dry?" Packy said, pulling at the seat of his pants before he sat down on the bench.

"You should sleep in your pants, like I do," Swede said. "That way your body heat dries them out."

Packy was about to answer back, but a look from Pa quieted them both down. The swampy smell of wet wool rose from the tables. Some of the fellows stunk so bad that Ben figured their clothes must be getting moldy.

Two jacks quit that day. The push, who normally got angry when men left in midseason, said, "I might quit myself if I didn't have to run this soggy outfit."

THE TWO-DAY BLOW

When cool weather returned, the mood of the camp immediately improved. Even Pa relaxed a little bit. One afternoon he said, "Why don't you boys show me that scone recipe of yours?"

"Are you serious?" Ben said. "What, did somebody die?"

Pa smiled. "I was serious last time, but that trick with Slim went over so good, I plumb forgot to follow up on the scone making. The jacks liked 'em so much, it will be a nice treat."

"Should I write the recipe down for you?" Ben asked.

"You know I don't believe in putting recipes on paper. I like 'em right here"—Pa tapped his temple—"where I can't lose 'em. You boys start in and I'll watch."

Ben and Nevers baked up forty extra scones this time, but the jacks were so hungry that all two hundred forty disappeared.

The change in weather brought both good news and bad news. The good news was that the roads firmed up and the trees stopped dripping like leaky faucets. The bad news was that a snowstorm blew in ahead of the cold front.

Ben was driving the swingdingle back from the cut on the afternoon the snow began. The wind had switched to the north early that morning. Dan's hooves crunched with every step, and the sleigh runners made a crackling sound as they skimmed over the ice crust. The snow started with the same wispy flakes that had been falling all winter, but as the wind picked up, the snow was soon stinging Ben's cheeks. By the time he had unloaded the swingdingle, the storm had turned into an all-out blow.

A short while later Day stopped by the cookshack and asked, "You mind if I borrow your cookees to help me hook up the snowplow?"

Ben had to blink to see as he and Nevers waded through the the calf-deep snow and helped hitch an eight-horse team to the log plow. "We may have to add another pair," Day hollered over the wind. "I'll take a swing and see how it goes."

That afternoon Ben visited with Charlie. Lately, he and Charlie had been talking about *Le Morte d'Arthur.* By reading a few minutes on Sunday afternoons, Ben had got through most of the story. He thought the saddest part was when King Arthur's loyal knight Lancelot fell in love with Queen Guinevere.

"Don't be too hard on Lancelot," Charlie said. "Arthur deserves a share of the blame for leaving his wife alone."

In the middle of a conversation about Camelot, Charlie's eyes lit up. "That reminds me of an autumn afternoon when Lucy and I hired a carriage," he said. "We had a picnic beside that waterfall north of town. She brought along a loaf of bread and a book of Shakespeare's sonnets. I furnished some wine and cheese. As we took turns reading those poems, the mist above the falls was lit with little floating rainbows. That was about the most peaceful moment I've ever spent on this earth."

○ ○ ○

That evening while Ben and Nevers were setting out the dinner plates, Day stopped by for a cup a coffee. The wind was still blowing so hard that the teamster had to hang on to the door latch as he shook the snow off his cap.

"Jiggers is taking a turn with the plow," Day said. His face looked like it had been rubbed with sandpaper.

"Are you keeping up?" Pa asked.

"So far, but we're up to a dozen-horse hitch."

When the rest of the teamsters came in for dinner, their faces were chafed as badly as Day's. Packy blew on his hands. "We sure got rid of that warm spell. Looks like a man's got to be careful what he wishes for."

A SUNDAY FLING

When Ben woke up the next morning, he felt something was wrong. He lay there for a moment until he realized the strange feeling came from the quiet. For the first time in two days the wind wasn't whistling through the stovepipe. Other than the deep breathing of Nevers, the world was perfectly still.

Just then Ben heard a scraping sound. Pa was already up and shoveling. Ben stoked the woodstove and hurried out to help. In the yellow glow of Pa's lantern, a few soft flakes were still sifting down, but the stars overhead hinted that a clear day was coming.

"You're up early," Pa said.

"The quiet woke me," Ben said.

"Me too." Pa pointed to the wall. "I got out a second shovel in case one of you laggards woke up. But you'd better check the temperature first."

It seemed silly to bother with taking the temperature on such a mild morning, but the push had made it clear that this was Ben's job until next month.

Ben had just put his thermometer away when Packy pulled into the yard and climbed off the plow. His horses hung their heads and blew puffs of steam. "I didn't hear no breakfast horn," Pa said.

"I know it ain't time yet," Packy said. "I was just wondering if Ben could take a turn plowing. I got to nap before I go out to the cut, or I ain't gonna be worth a darn."

At first Ben thought Packy was joking, but he didn't laugh like the push had last fall when he'd teased Ben about driving the team. "Can I, Pa?" Ben asked.

"I suppose me and Nevers can start the cooking."

Packy showed Ben where to stand on the front of the plow. "Brace yourself when they start," he said. "One swing down to the river and back and we'll have her all cleared. Needlenose'll help you sort out the team when you're done. These hay burners deserve a rest." Packy walked off to the bunkhouse.

Knowing that Day's leaders were in front, Ben picked up the reins and said, "Walk, boys." Despite Packy's warning, the rig nearly pitched him off when it jerked forward. But once the horses plodded past the cookshack and turned up the road, the big V plow skimmed smoothly over the ice ruts and pushed the snowbanks back on both sides.

Ben looked up at the last few stars sparkling above the pines. Steam rose from the backs of the horses, and frost flakes settled on their shaggy manes. He enjoyed listening to the jingling of the harness chains, which matched the rhythm of the team.

By the time he had finished the river loop and pulled back into camp, the jacks were arriving for breakfast. "What's this?" Jiggers said. "Has our cookee turned into a teamster overnight?"

Packy, who'd finished his nap, nodded. "Ben's doing so many jobs around camp, we're gonna have to call him Blackwater Ben."

The other men smiled, but just when Ben was ready to feel proud, Swede said, "Since you like chasing after Old Dan so much, I'm surprised you ain't running behind that plow instead of driving it." Then the other fellows all laughed.

On the day after the storm Ben got a letter from Mrs. Wilson. Nevers was even more anxious than Ben to see what she had written, especially when he saw that the letter was two full pages.

Dear Benjamin,

I think of you often and how hard it must be to keep those hungry lumberjacks fed. The chickadees are still enjoying your bird feeder, though a nasty shrike has taken to lunching on the unsuspecting twitterers lately. I'd have Harley shoot that rapacious bird, but I don't know if he'd have the brains to put the bullets in the right end of the gun.

Winter has been rather dull around here. The only item of interest occurred on the final day of that warm spell—we had a thaw here in Blackwater just like you described in your letter.

The unseasonable weather woke a bear out of hibernation, and he wandered into town in the middle of the afternoon. The local folks, knowing that bears are mean and hungry when they come out of their dens too early, all gave him a wide berth.

The bear was minding his own business when a saloon girl stepped into the street. Not being accustomed to bears and having just woken up herself, she panicked and pulled a little derringer out of her garter belt. A few of the fellows yelled, "Don't," from the other side of the street, but it was too late. She fired that toy pistol right into the bear's behind.

The bear could have turned and chewed her to pieces—it would have served her right—but he sprinted for the river instead. As luck would have it, he ran right toward Maggie Montgomery's backyard. Maggie was hanging her sheets on the line at the time. When she heard the derringer go off, she called over the clothesline to our house, "Was that a gunshot, Evy?"

I said, "It sounded more like a fire—" but before I could get "cracker" out, I saw the bear running along the top of the hill. Knowing that poor Maggie was in a fragile state of mind, I was glad to see that the bear was going to miss her by a wide margin. But that very minute my unhandy handyman, Harley, banged the cellar door.

The startled bear swerved and got caught up in Maggie's sheets. The next thing I knew, Maggie was shrieking like her heart was being cut out, and she and the clothesline and the sheets and the bear were all tangled together and rolling down the hill.

I suspect it will take Maggie a long while to recover from this incident. So don't forget her in your prayers.

Sincerely yours,

Mrs. E. Wilson

P.S. Let me know when you are coming home, Ben, and I will give that dunderhead Harley his walking papers.

P.P.S. And please remind Mr. Harrigan that his unsolicited comments regarding my private correspondence are not appreciated.

As usual, Nevers enjoyed the letter, and Charlie laughed out loud when Ben showed him the paragraph about Maggie and the bear. "I would certainly like to meet Mrs. Wilson someday," Charlie said. "In your next letter tell her that I consider her privacy of the utmost importance and I will refrain from further commentary."

"Will you help me with the spelling?"

"Of course."

o o o

For the next two weeks the weather settled into a perfect pattern for hauling. The cold nights and cool days allowed the teamsters to make up for the days they'd missed by running their sleds twenty-four hours a day. "Does it look like we'll be making the contract now?" Ben asked Pa.

"As long as the weather holds, I'd say so."

"And it's about time we got a break," the push said. "For once it ain't either too cold or too hot. I suppose we'll be getting hit by a tornado or a hurricane any day now."

"You shouldn't never wish a hurricane to come, sir," Nevers said. "Pardon me for speaking up. But I lost my favorite uncle when the storm surge of a big ole 'cane washed his house away."

"I was only joking," the push said.

"I know, sir," Nevers said.

o o o

A few days later Ben and Nevers were getting the lunch together when Ben heard something. "Listen," he said, and ran to the door. Nevers was only a step behind. Water was dripping off the eaves again.

"This time we got us a real thaw," Ben said.

"Spring is finally here," Nevers agreed.

"What are you two yelling about?" Pa walked up behind them. "By golly, those snowbanks have shrunk since breakfast."

"You think the bottom'll fall out of the roads?" Ben asked.

"It takes a while to melt the ice," Pa said. "But I expect the boys will only be hauling at night from now on."

When Ben and Nevers headed down to the bunkhouse the next Sunday, Ben was surprised to see the men milling around outside. Packy had a double-bitted ax in his hand, and he was walking away from the bunkhouse. "Eight, nine, ten," he said. "That makes ten paces." He laid a stick down in the slush. "Who wants to go first?" Jiggers was drawing a charcoal circle on the butt end of a bunkhouse log for a target.

"I'll give her a try," Arno said.

After being cooped up all winter, Ben could see that the jacks intended to have a little fun. As Arno hefted the ax in one hand, the men teased him. "Be careful, Arno," Packy said. "That blade is a whole lot sharper than a horseshoe hammer."

Arno closed one eye and aimed at the target. "We'll see about that," he said. He lifted the ax above his shoulder once, and again. Then he sent it whirling toward the log.

When the ax hit the log sideways, splintering the hickory handle, the jacks all roared.

"You'd better stick with your hammer and tongs," Day called.

"You're supposed to hit the log with the sharp end, Mr. Iron Burner," Jiggers cackled.

"Shut yer faces," Arno growled. "Give me another ax."

Packy handed Arno a second ax, and this time he threw more quickly. He missed the corner of the bunkhouse, and the ax bounced handle first off the side of the outhouse.

The men laughed even louder.

Just then the door of the outhouse opened and Windy stepped out with his pants at half-mast. "What are you hooligans doing out here?"

Windy flipped the ax back and cussed everyone out. The louder he cussed, the more the fellows howled. Windy couldn't figure out what was so funny until he looked down and saw that his pants were at his ankles. Ben laughed until his sides ached.

Though a few fellows buried the ax in the log, no one hit the black circle. Pa even tried a couple of throws. When Packy said, "Does Blackwater Ben want to try a toss?" Ben stepped forward. He missed the bull's-eye, but he was happy that the ax stuck in the wood instead of cutting a hunk of tar paper off the eave like Nevers's throw did.

The contest finally came down to Packy and Slim. Though Packy hit the edge of the charcoal circle with his blade, Slim did him one better by burying his throw just inside the mark. The fellows cheered.

When the ax throwing was done, Arno said, "Let's try a man's game."

"Like square dancing?" Jiggers hooted.

"Come over here," Arno replied, scowling. He led the men to his blacksmith's shop. The double doors were propped open, and sunlight streamed into the smoke-blackened interior. The stained oak floor was littered with burnt pieces of iron and with wood shavings that had been tracked over from the wood butcher's work area. Thin wisps of smoke rose from the cold forge.

Arno walked over to his anvil. "Let's see you try this," he said. Bending at the waist, Arno put both of his fore-arms under the anvil and heaved upward. To Ben's aston-ishment, he lifted it straight up and shuffled forward with the steel pressed against his belly. Arno carried the anvil all the way to the carpenter's bench and set it down. "Now, there's a man's labor," he said, dusting off his hands. "Who's next?"

Most of the men just shook their heads. Day managed to lift the anvil, but before he got halfway to the forge, he dropped it. Ben was proud that of the three other fellows who tried, Pa got the farthest of anyone.

Then Swede said, "What sort of child's game is this?" He stepped forward and picked up the anvil. Marching past the forge to the door, he pitched the anvil over the threshold. The base buried itself six inches deep in the mud. "There," he said.

Later that afternoon Arno and a few fellows were tak-ing turns arm wrestling at a table inside the bunkhouse. Ben expected the blacksmith to beat everyone, but after a long battle, Day finally put Arno's wrist down.

Swede laughed.

"Want to give it a shot?" Day rubbed his biceps.

"Get up," he said.

Looking confused, Day and Arno stood. Ben wondered if Swede was going to pick up the table and throw it out the door. Instead, he placed his hands on his knees and bent down. Then he clamped his teeth on the edge of the table. Ben heard the wood crunch as Swede's jaws closed.

Every fellow in the shack gasped as Swede lifted the table up. The card players crowded forward for a better view.

"Well, I ain't never . . . ," Windy whispered, rubbing his jaw as if it hurt to watch.

Swede shifted his hands to his hips as he carried the table all the way to the doorway. When he finally relaxed his bite, the table crashed to the floor, rattling the planking.

The men sat in stunned silence as Swede said, "That's better exercise than holding hands."

The late-season success of the hauling crews lightened Pa's mood. One bright morning when Ben took down the Gabriel horn and gave it to Pa, Pa handed it back to him. "Why don't you give her a try?" he said.

"Me?" Ben said.

Pa pushed open the door. "Just press your lips together and let her go."

Ben lifted the long horn and puffed. A tiny squeak came out.

"Blow from down here." Pa pointed below his chest.

This time a sharp squeal echoed over the clearing.

Packy stuck his head out the bunkhouse door. "Are you calling us for breakfast, Blackwater? Or are you trying to lure a lovesick moose?" Ben heard the fellows laughing inside.

"Don't pay them no heed," Pa said. "You'll catch on."

The next morning Ben figured Pa would call the men himself, but he handed the horn to Ben again. Though the sound was still squeaky, he got better volume. And by the third day he was making a passable bugle blast.

"You're gonna be a fine bugler," Pa said. "By next season you'll be playing reveille."

Next season, Ben thought. That was the first time Pa had mentioned that he might want him working as a cookee again. But Ben had already decided that if he worked in a logging camp another winter, he was going to do his best to get himself a teamstering job.

THE PROMISE OF TOWN

Over the next few weeks camp life wound down quickly. Once the Blackwater Company had completed its contract, Ben was amazed at how fast the logging operation shut down. The jacks left in the same order they had been hired. The first men to go were the sawyers and skid men, followed by the loaders and teamsters and road monkeys. One by one the fellows tied their turkeys together and stopped by the clerk's shack to collect their pay slips. The last to go were the blacksmith and wood butcher, who were busy with end-of-the-season repairs.

On the day Packy left he took Nevers aside. "You know all that French cussing I abused you with?"

Nevers tensed up like he was getting ready for Packy to broadside him with another French oath.

"Well, I wasn't swearing at all."

"I don't believe you."

"Do you call *Don't count your chickens before they hatch* cussing?"

"What?"

"That's how *En Avril ne te découvre pas d'un fil* translates."

"Are you kidding me?"

Jiggers punched Nevers in the arm. "Ole Pack sure had you goin', didn't he?"

"But what about those other things you were saying?"

"Like *Tout ce qui brille n'est pas or?*"

Nevers nodded.

"That means *All that glitters is not gold.* Just like *Mieux vaut tard que jamais* is the same as saying *Better late than never*, and *Vivre et laisser vivre* only means *Live and let live*. But my favorite is *Il faut savoir tirer parti du pire—If you are dealt a lemon, make lemonade.*"

"But you made them all sound like cuss words."

"You heard what you wanted to." Packy extended his hand to Nevers. "No hard feelings?"

"No hard feelings," Nevers said, shaking his hand.

Packy and Jiggers climbed into the tote teamster's wagon and slipped their turkeys off their shoulders. Then, just as the horses started forward, Packy grinned slyly and called to Nevers: *"Tout va bien qui finit bien!"*

Nevers threw down his cap and swore.

The day after Packy and Jiggers had left, the camp got strangely quiet. Ben was surprised when Pa said, "I sorta miss that little Frenchman."

"You do?" Ben said.

"He and his partner might have been noisy, but they were good company and steady woodsmen. As lousy as the weather was this year, they did a fine job of getting the timber out."

The day after the teamsters and loaders left camp, Windy stopped by the cookshack in the middle of the morning. "Well, Benny Boy," he said, "it's time for me to get that new set of choppers."

"Who's gonna take care of the bunkhouse?"

"The handful of fellows who are left can sweep up on their own. The push told me that the dentist in Duluth is so good that you can't tell the difference between the teeth he makes up and the good Lord's."

"Good luck," Ben said.

"I'll be back with my new choppers in a few days. You just be ready to fry me up a big juicy steak."

"I'll be waiting."

Soon the only men left in camp other than the cookshack crew were the push, the clerk, the wood butcher, and the dentist. With the lighter workload everyone was a lot more relaxed. When Ben stopped by the clerk's office to buy a pocketknife, the pencil pusher actually smiled. "So you're gonna treat yourself to a present after your long winter of hard work?"

"I lost my old one," Ben said.

"Those knives have a way of walking off," Wally said

as he marked down Ben's purchase in his ledger. "Looks like you haven't wasted much cash, according to my book. You'll have a good stake coming."

Ben was surprised when the pencil pusher leaned on the counter and asked, "You figure on signing up for our river drive next month?"

"Really?" Ben had been hinting all winter that he'd like to be hired as a log driver, but Wally hadn't said a word. "You suppose Nevers could go, too?"

"We can always use a couple of river rats to help us ride those logs downstream."

"Don't you go hiring away my cookee as a log driver." Ben turned. Pa standing was in the doorway. "Now that Ben Ward has finally learned his way around the kitchen, I don't want nobody drowning him."

Pa was complimenting him?

"Blackwater Ben!" someone shouted.

Ben looked out the door, but all he could see was the tote teamster driving toward the cookshack. Then a face peered over the back of the wagon seat. "Benny Boy! How's our swingdingle driver doing?"

It was Windy.

Ben and Nevers helped the bull cook climb out of the wagon and limp up the steps of the bunkhouse. Windy was toothless and bootless and looked like he'd been dragged a mile through the mud.

"What about your big plans?" Ben asked as Windy sat down on the first deacon's bench.

"Not so many questions, Benny Boy." Windy raised

one hand like he was trying to push back the memory of the last three days. "When I got to Blackwater, I went straight to the depot like I'd promised myself. But I met an old buddy named Scott Hull. He offered me a whiskey, and I couldn't refuse. I told him I'd just have one." Windy hung his head. "The next thing I knew I'd blowed my whole stake, tooth money and all."

"But what happened to your boots?" Nevers asked.

"Boots?" Windy looked down at his mud-encrusted socks. "Danged if I know."

Ben was still shaking his head when he and Nevers got back to the cookshack.

"How could Windy waste a whole year's salary in one weekend?" Ben asked Pa.

"I warned you it would turn out this way."

"But he had such great hopes."

"It's not like he planned for it to happen. These jacks live for the moment. They never stop to think of next week or next year. I'm sure Windy meant to take only one drink."

"But why can't he change?"

"Don't forget there's a good side to these fellows, too," Pa said. "Most men go through life pinching pennies and paying on mortgages that they have no hope of finishing off. But these jacks don't owe nobody nothing. They go where they want when they want to. Their lives are their own, free and clear."

Ben still couldn't help shaking his head.

"So, you figure on helping me with the wanigan when the spring drive starts?" Pa asked.

Ben looked at Pa and then at Nevers. "Me and Nevers are thinking of signing on as log drivers."

"That's right, Mr. Ward," Nevers said, beaming. "As light as I am, I figure I should be able to ride a log down a white-water rapids and not even get my bootlaces wet."

"You boys won't want to be out on that freezing river when you could be staying dry inside the wanigan with me." Pa turned back to his work.

"We're set on trying it, Pa," Ben said.

"What's that?" Pa looked up.

Ben took a deep breath. "After cooking all winter, Nevers and I have decided that we're ready for a change. Running the river is what we aim to do."

For a moment Pa looked like he was ready to chew Ben out. Nevers took a nervous step backward, but Ben looked Pa straight in the eye.

"You're serious, ain't you?" Pa said.

Ben nodded.

"Well, then." Pa shifted his gaze from Ben to Nevers. "I reckon we'll have to be fitting you boys for some calk boots."

◉ ◉ ◉

On April first, Ben and Nevers were helping Pa pack up the last of the kitchen utensils. "We better get out of here before the rains start," Pa said. "Once mud time comes, our wagon will be stuck here till next month."

"So where you staying between now and the river drive?" Ben asked Nevers.

"I figure I'll rent me a place in town."

"You suppose Mrs. Wilson would have room?" Ben looked at Pa.

"She's usually full up in the spring," Pa said, "but you'd be welcome to bunk with us."

"Really?" Nevers said.

Ben grinned. "Us cookees got to stick together, don't we?"

Later that morning Ben was carrying some supplies out of the root cellar when he heard music. There'd been lots of birds twittering in the brush lately, but this didn't sound like birdsong. Ben walked toward the cookshack and stopped. Someone was singing in a deep baritone voice.

Just then Windy ran from the bunkhouse. "He's boiling up!" Windy shouted. "I swear he's boiling up."

"What's goin' on?" Pa stepped outside.

"It's the dentist." Windy paused to catch his breath. "He's gone to the boiling-up shack, and he's cleaning himself up."

Nevers came to the door, too.

"I'll be jiggered." Pa looked over Nevers's head.

Charlie was strolling toward the cookshack. He was freshly shaven, and he was wearing black pants and a white shirt. He carried a towel over his arm.

"Top of the morning," Charlie said when he reached the cookshack steps.

It took Pa a moment to find his voice, but he finally said, "Morning."

Nevers's eyes bugged out. "You got a chin!"

Everyone laughed as Charlie touched his cheek and said, "Did you think my whiskers were hanging on air?"

"So whatever brought you outta your shack?" Pa asked.

"Young Benjamin convinced me that I'd been misinterpreting the ending of a famous piece of literature."

Pa gave Ben a long look. "If Ben has a knack for figuring out stories, he got it from his mother."

"That may very well be true." Charlie rested his foot on the step and looked up at Pa. "I've been meaning to have a talk with you and the squire. Your cooking got me through the winter. I know it's a bit early for teatime, but would you chaps have a cup of swamp water handy?

"Teatime?" Pa frowned.

"That's Newcastle upon Tyne talk, Pa," Ben said.

"Squire Benjamin is correct," Charlie said. "And is there any chance that you gentlemen might have scones on the menu this afternoon?"

"We're fresh out of scones," Ben said, "but we may be able to scrounge up a piece of lemon pie."

"That happens to be one of my favorites," Charlie said, putting his arm around Ben and walking through the door.

"Mine too," Ben said.

"I'll fetch some cups," Nevers said. "You fellers have yourselves a seat."

"Thanks, son," Charlie said, choosing a bench near the open door.

"That sun sure does feel good," Pa said.

"The longer the winter, the more we appreciate

spring," Charlie said. He paused for a moment, then looked at Ben. "Has young Benjamin told you that we have a mutual acquaintance?"

Pa shook his head as Nevers set cups of tea in front of everyone.

"Charlie knew Mother, Pa," Ben said.

"What's that?" Pa frowned as he took a sip of tea.

"Charlie courted her before you did."

Pa stared at Ben, still frowning. "I tried to tell you, Pa. But you wouldn't never listen."

Pa turned to Charlie, and his eyebrows rose. "Of course!" he said. "You must be that musical Englishman everyone was talking about when I first moved to town. The boys told me about a fancy-dressed fellow who'd been hanging around Lucy."

"That would be me," Charlie said.

"It sure is a small world." Pa shook his head. "I heard you got so mad one day that you stripped off all your clothes and threw them into the river."

"People do exaggerate." Charlie chuckled. "The only garment I discarded was my coat."

After a moment of silence, Ben said, "Well, you can't say Charlie didn't have good taste in women, eh, Pa?"

Pa blinked, and then he smiled. "No. No, I can't." He turned to Charlie. "This calls for a toast." Pa raised his teacup, and so did Charlie.

"Most certainly," Charlie said. He looked at the boys. "Will you join us, chaps?"

Ben and Nevers nodded, and everyone leaned forward

so they could clink their tin cups together. "To Lucy Ward," said Pa, and the boys echoed him.

"To Lucinda," Charlie said.

They were quiet for a moment again. Then Charlie smiled and asked Pa, "Did you ever hear about the time I hired a fiddler to play outside Lucy's school window?"

Pa shook his head.

"It was September, and the students were still restless from their summer holiday. So I—".

Just then the tote teamster poked his head in the door and called to Charlie, "You comin'?"

"Blimey! Is it that time already?"

"Yep."

Charlie shook Nevers's and Pa's hands. Then he turned to Ben. "You behave yourself, squire. And if you ever decide to swap your swingdingle driving for inside work, I'd be happy to show you the tricks of the filer's trade."

"My heart's in teamstering right now." Ben squeezed Charlie's hand. "But I can see where it would be nice to stay close to the stove when it's fifty below."

Then Pa said, "We'll have to continue our visit sometime, Charlie. I imagine that Ben would like hearing more about his ma." Ben and Nevers stared at Pa in disbelief. "I've got some stories of my own to tell, along with a few silver mining tales."

"I'm sure that we can put our heads together and dredge up a few memories," Charlie said. "In the meantime, I plan to call on a certain widow lady who has a reputation for appreciating the art of conversation." Charlie winked at Ben.

○ ○ ○

Later that afternoon Ben noticed something lying on his bunk. He picked it up and sank down on his blanket. It was Charlie's photograph of Ben's mother. Charlie had carved a birch frame for the photograph and left a note beside it:

Greetings, Squire.
     You deserve to have this picture on your wall more than I do. Besides, it's time for me to be moving on.
     I'll wager a fiver that when you show this to your pa, he'll be able to think of lots more stories to tell you.

                    Cheerio,
                    Charles Harrigan

P.S. If things work out with Mrs. You-Know-Who, I may see you soon. If not—you and Nevers stay dry on your river drive.

AFTERWORD

Imagine a four-horse team harnessed in tandem and hitched to a thirty-foot-high sled load of logs weighing 140 tons. Sounds impossible? On February 26, 1893, in northern Minnesota, four horses pulled such a load three miles to a landing, where it was later transported on nine railroad flatcars to the World's Fair in Chicago. That single load scaled out to a total of 36,055 board feet—enough wood to build ten modern homes. Over the years true reports of such gargantuan feats mingled with tall tales, eventually leading to the creation of mythic figures such as Paul Bunyan and his companion, Babe, the blue ox.

○ ○ ○

But where did America's storied lumberjack traditions begin? Logging has always played a central role in the history of America. Long before the American Revolution, scouts of the British Royal Navy claimed New England's tallest and straightest trees in the name of the crown by blazing them with a broad arrow mark. A Surveyor General of the King's Woods was appointed to protect these trees—some of which were more than two hundred feet tall, and perfect for ships' masts—but it was impossible to stop the local citizens from cutting them down.

Lumber was not only important for building farms, schools, and churches in Colonial America, but it was also exported in large quantities. Besides providing materials for shipbuilding and cabinetmaking, American lumber was used to manufacture heading and barrel staves. Hogsheads were shipped to the West Indies as molasses containers, while barrels were used to ship apples and potatoes. Wooden lime casks were also in great demand. Milled lumber was traded for gold, rum, and molasses throughout the Caribbean. Cuba used 40 million board feet of American lumber in a single year for sugar boxes.

As settlers moved farther west, the forest was regarded as an impediment to progress. Trees were chopped, girdled, and burned to make way for houses and farms. Everyone assumed that the vast timber reserves were inexhaustible. However, by 1839 loggers had cut their way through the pine stands of Maine, Michigan, and Wisconsin and arrived in Minnesota (then a part of the Wisconsin Territory).

Experienced lumbermen traveled from New England to start the first sawmill in the St. Croix River Valley, and within a decade the community of Stillwater, Minnesota, became the lumber milling center for the whole territory. As the demand for lumber increased, logging camps spread north toward the Canadian border. By the 1860s mills in Stillwater and Minneapolis had switched from circular saws to steam-powered band saws, and their increased efficiency allowed them to supply America's growing need for railroad ties and dimensional lumber. Minnesota wood was soon being marketed from New York to Denver.

In 1900, the peak year of white pine production in Minnesota, 20,000 men and 10,000 horses were employed at lumber camps in the north woods. Using only axes and crosscut saws to fell trees that were often too large for two men to reach around the middle, the lumberjacks harvested 2.3 billion board feet of timber. Enough pine was cut in 1900 alone to build 600,000 two-story homes. That lumber sawed into one-foot-wide boards and placed end to end could have stretched all the way from the earth to the moon!

Soon the white pine reserves, which had been regarded as endless, came to a sudden end. Trees were cut so rapidly that timber production began to decrease as early as 1901. Yet the logging continued. The largest white pine sawmill in the world operated in Virginia, Minnesota, from 1910 to 1929. Every twenty-four hours the Virginia Rainy Lake Company sawed 500,000 board feet of lumber, producing more than 2 billion board feet of lumber and lath in its twenty-year life.

By 1930 the largest logging companies had left Minnesota and headed west, seeking richer stands of timber. Yet the cutting of white pine still went on. Today only 2 percent of the original 3.5 million acres of white pine remain. Except in remote areas such as the Boundary Waters Canoe Area Wilderness and the Chippewa National Forest's "Lost Forty" north of Grand Rapids, Minnesota, old-growth pine

KITCHEN OF A MINNESOTA LUMBER CAMP CA. 1900

is extremely rare. Minnesota once had twice as much white pine as New Hampshire, but it presently has less than one twentieth as much.

Attempts at reforestation have been complicated by white pine blister rust disease, deer feeding, and modern timbering, which relies on faster-growing species such as aspen. Groups such as the White Pine Society hope that the white pine can be restored, but their funding is limited. Despite these problems, people remain hopeful that with dedication and hard work, Minnesotans can one day help these four-hundred-year-old crown jewels reclaim their rightful place in the forest.

What was it like for the men who worked in the woods back in the lumberjack days?

Though the normal load for the logging sleds wasn't as large as the 140-ton show load that was put together for the World's Fair, four-horse teams typically hauled 20 to 25 tons of wood at a time. The reason such enormous weight could be moved by horses was the system of ice roads that logging camps employed. When the roads were first swamped—or cleared—the grade was carefully calculated to allow for mainly downhill pulls to the landings. Since logging was done only in the winter, a sled-mounted water tank iced the roads to give the runners maximum slippage, and a bull rutter cut grooves into the ice.

As hard as the horses worked in the logging camps, the lumberjacks worked even harder. In fact, most logging camp foremen were more concerned about the health of the horses than that of the jacks, who they believed could take anything.

The jacks, who were infamously crabby fellows, tolerated bitterly cold temperatures and long hours in the woods, but they demanded good food. No matter what the wages, jacks always asked who the cook was before they signed on at a camp. Lumberjacks ate an astonishing 5,000 to 6,000 calories per day.

Once spring came, the logs were shipped to sawmills by railcar, or they were driven downriver when the ice went out. On the larger lakes, steamboats pulled huge booms of logs across the open water to railheads and mills. River drives usually began in mid-April in Minnesota and lasted about six weeks.

Lack of winter snow cover or spring rains could make it difficult or impossible to drive the logs to the mill. High water could also cause problems by allowing the logs to float over the riverbanks and become stranded. The men who rode the logs downriver were called river pigs. It took great skill and courage to balance on a log that could easily tip a man into the freezing cold water. A flat-bottomed wanigan boat, a combination floating cookshack and bunkhouse that could accommodate twenty men, accompanied the men on their downriver journey.

Logjams presented the most dangerous obstacle to the river drives. It took great skill for a river pig to identify and remove a key log that could be holding back several million feet of timber. Dynamite was sometimes used to break the logs free, but the job usually fell to a single man who walked out onto the jam and pried or pulled the key log loose. When the logjam broke, many a man was lost as he attempted to run across the crashing logs to the riverbank.

Once the winter logging season was done and the drives were completed, loggers often squandered their wages on a single weekend in town. While a few of the more responsible men saved their money and invested in farms and other businesses, jacks tended to live for the day and not give much thought to anything except getting back under the tar paper again when the next logging season started.

LOGGING HISTORY RESOURCES

The best way to learn about the early days of logging is to talk with real lumberjacks. If there aren't any lumberjacks in your neighborhood, listening to oral history tapes of loggers is a handy substitute. Tapes and transcripts are available at many university libraries, historical societies, and forest history centers. There are also many good books and articles on logging. The following resources will help you get started:

BOOKS

Daylight in the Swamp by Robert W. Wells, NorthWord Press, Inc., Minocqua, Wisconsin (1978).

Early Loggers in Minnesota, Volumes I–IV by J. C. Ryan, Minnesota Timber Producers Association, Duluth (1973–1986).

History of the White Pine Industry in Minnesota by Agnes Larson, Arno Press, New York (1972).

Holy Old Mackinaw: A Natural History of the American Lumberjack by Stewart H. Holbrook, Macmillan, New York (1956).

The Loggers by Richard Williams, Little, Brown & Company, New York (1976).

The Maine Woods by Henry David Thoreau, Penguin USA, New York (1988).

Tall Timber: A Pictorial History of Logging in the Upper Midwest by Tom Bacig and Fred Thompson, Voyageur Press, Bloomington, Minnesota (1982).

Timber! by Ben Rajala, North Star Press, St. Cloud, Minnesota (1991).

Under the Tarpaper by J. C. Ryan, St. Louis County Historical Society, Duluth, Minnesota (1985).

ORGANIZATIONS

Cradle of Forestry in America (CFAIA)
100 S. Broad St.
Brevard, NC 28712
Phone: (800) 660-0671 or (828) 884-5713
E-mail: cfaia@citcom.net
Web site: www.cradleofforestry.com

Forest History Center
2609 County Road 76
Grand Rapids, MN 55744
Phone: (218) 327-4482
E-mail: foresthistory@mnhs.org
Web site: www.mnhs.org/places/sites/fhc

Forest History Society
701 Wm. Vickers Ave.
Durham, NC 27701-3162
Phone: (919) 682-9319
E-mail: recluce2@duke.edu
Web site: www.lib.duke.edu/forest

Minnesota Historical Society
345 W. Kellogg Blvd.
St. Paul, MN 55102-1906
Phone: (651) 296-6126
E-mail: reference@mnhs.org
Web site: www.mnhs.org

United States Department of Agriculture Forest Service
(USDA Forest Service)
P.O. Box 96090
Washington, D.C. 20090-6090
Phone: (202) 205-8333
E-mail: webmaster@fs.fed.us
Web site: www.fs.fed.us

World Forestry Center
4033 SW Canyon Rd.
Portland, OR 97221
Phone: (503) 228-1367
E-mail: mail@worldforestry.org
Web site: www.worldforestry.org